TALKING TO GHOSTS AT PARTIES

"Told with honesty and wry humour, and with elements of magical realism and the fantastical, these stories also detail the absurdity in the mundane. This idiosyncratic collection is a joy to read."

– *Lucie McKnight Hardy* –

Author of Dead Relatives

"Talking to Ghosts at Parties is a fantastic glimpse into the absurd that travels the full spectrum of human emotion. White's stories are full of a cool intelligence and razor-sharp wit whisking readers from banal reality to wild surrealism and back again. Infused with wry humor, shrewd observations, punk rock sensibility and great heart, this collection embraces characters existing on the fringes of society."

– *Sara Dobbie* –

Author of Flight Instinct

"Rick White is a very smart guy. He's also a very funny guy. And the stories in this collection are just like him: very smart and very funny. Sometimes they're sad, too. Sometimes they're smart and sad and funny. And sometimes, you look up from the ghost you've been talking to at this party, and realize it has been your reflection all along. And these stories, these smart and funny and sometimes sad stories, are holding up a mirror and showing us the reflection of everyone we know. This is a very smart collection. And Rick White is a very smart guy."

– *Cathy Ulrich* –

Author of Ghosts of You

"What a joy to see these stories collected together at last. White moves effortlessly between voices, sexes, ages and perspectives with eloquent empathy, strong storytelling and deft comic timing. But the humour never punches down, and these tales that shine a tender, unflinching light on the unseen, the marginalised and the hopelessly human are shot through with a fierce compassion."

– *Dan Brotzel* -

Author of The Wolf in the Woods

"Talking To Ghosts At Parties is a stunning debut collection from one of the most unique voices working in short fiction; and Rick White is only getting started – witty, dark, and memorable … a rollicking good read."

– *Ross Jeffery* –

Author of Bram Stoker Award-nominated Tome

"Each story is a delicious, mysterious morsel, a bite-sized offering of the wondrous, the odd, the surreal. Although Rick White's characters may look and sound like regular people, they are in fact outsiders and oddballs, struggling to make sense of their circumstances, their lives, other people, always only one slip-up away from revealing their true, transgressive selves. Like the character who lives in a tower of memories, they are all trapped in a prison of loneliness, so desperate to hide their essential deviancy from other people that they are too afraid to reach out, unable to comprehend that it is their extraordinary strangeness that makes them human."

– *Sian Hughes* –

Author of Pain Sluts

"Smart, sardonic, and thoroughly entertaining, Talking To Ghosts At Parties is a delight from start to finish, written by a master of flash fiction. In these pages, White has absolutely nailed both the art of dark humour and the art of the short form. The droll dialogue, the absurd circumstances, the cast of dysfunctional characters and the way their lives intertwine are all wickedly clever inventions by White, and make for a hilarious, riveting, incredibly satisfying read."

– *HLR* –

Author of History of Present Complaint

"An onslaught of provocative and mind-bending prose – Rick White delights with an ensemble of macabre and enriching stories that will make you think long after you've put the book down."

– *Anthony Self* –

Author of Birthday Treat

Also available from STORGY Books:

Exit Earth
Shallow Creek
Hopeful Monsters
You Are Not Alone
This Ragged, Wastrel Thing
Annihilation Radiation
Parade
Pain Sluts

STORGY®

BOOKS

STORGY® BOOKS Ltd.
London, United Kingdom, 2022

First Published in Great Britain in 2022 by STORGY® Books

London

Grateful acknowledgement is made to the following publications in which some of these stories were first published: ...

Published by STORGY® BOOKS Ltd.
London, United Kingdom, 2022

10 9 8 7 6 5 4 3 2 1

Cover Art by Rob Taylor
Cover Design by Tomek Dzido

Edited & Typeset by Tomek Dzido

A CIP catalogue record for this title is available from the British Library

Trade Paperback ISBN 978-1-7397350-0-5
eBook ISBN 978-1-7397350-1-2

www.storgy.com

TALKING TO GHOSTS AT PARTIES

STORIES FOR THE ORPHANS, THE OUTCASTS, AND THE STRANGE.

RICK WHITE

STORGY BOOKS

FOR SARAH

CONTENTS

Uncle Charlie's Bicycle	1
The Clampdown	5
Luxembourg	13
You'll Never Be A Cat	17
Dog-Face Malone, meet Linda	21
Infinite Growth	31
NO NON SWIMMERS BEYOND THIS POINT	41
Lycanthropy (Werewolf Kitchen)	45
A Beautiful Proof	57
Jam	59
Bees, motherfucker!	69
Eric the Astronomer	77
Troy (...or How to get to Penguin Island)	79
Cooping Mechanism	85
Pop music is the ideal music to run to	87
Cafeteria	93
The Only Way To Mansplain It	101
Stinky McGuirk	105
The Lost Art of Letter Writing	111
Crisis Actor	113
Lily	115
Staring at the Cabbages	121
In the place where all your old band mates go	123

CONTENTS

The Principle of Gentleness 133
Toast 137
Free to a Good Home 141
Crab Bucket 153
Trifle 157
F23 165
To Cloak 169

“YES, WE ARE OF GOOD COURAGE, AND WE WOULD RATHER BE AWAY FROM THE BODY AND AT HOME WITH THE LORD.”

- 2 CORINTHIANS 5:8 -

UNCLE CHARLIE'S BICYCLE

Esther lived in corners. Behind the backs of armchairs. In the black and white shadows cast by the TV which Ma sat in front of all day. Saturday afternoons were for wrestling—Ma's favourite—and the other kids, the other no-hoper-kids, the wards of the state, all gathered round to watch.

"That's The Black Bomber," Ma would shout. "Sergeant Nitro, The Masked Intruder," she would shriek and holler from her sunken nicotine throne, haloed in cigarette smoke—powder blue and sulphurous yellow.

Esther was a mark, a low-carder, the perpetual victim of the rowdy, hyped-up boys and their fighting ways. *Clotheslines*, *DDTs*, *backbreakers*, *German suplexes*, *powerslams* and *piledrivers*, all meted out on thin mattresses and worn-out sofas. "Roughhousing," Ma called it.

To Esther, the names of all the moves sounded like fear, tasted metallic, like the cat spatula which Ma used to make scrambled eggs on a Sunday and to fling pieces of shit out the cat's litter tray into the yard.

Esther liked the cat though. His name was Arnold and, well, he'd curl up at the foot of Esther's bed, on the rare nights when no one came. In the pitch black of her windowless bedroom she could still make out the gleam of Arnold's eyes in the darkness. It was nice to know he was there. Arnold was her tag-team partner.

When there was no wrestling on TV, and when Ma took to drinking (which was most days), Ma liked to pick two kids to fight in front of her. She'd make everyone gather round and chant, "FIGHT! FIGHT! FIGHT!" while the two chosen contestants duked it out. Ma knew which kids had a mean streak, and she knew which ones didn't really want to fight. So she'd put them together. Said it was "character building" for the weaker kids. Ma liked to be entertained, so you'd better look as though you were trying and make it a good fight, otherwise you'd be in even worse trouble.

When Esther was picked, she made a show of whirling her arms around to try and land a blow, but she rarely succeeded and was always pinned eventually. Esther had come to know, only too well, that it's damn near impossible to shift the weight of a teenage boy once he's lying on top of you.

"Quit daydreaming and fetch Uncle Charlie's bicycle," said Ma one afternoon. Esther flinched at the sound of Ma's words—they all sounded like wrestling moves. "Then get your ass to the store and get me a fifth of bourbon and a carton of smokes." Esther wasn't sure what those things were.

Uncle Charlie lived next door. He wasn't Esther's real uncle any more than Ma was her real ma. Uncle Charlie was something called a "Handy Man", which sounded to Esther like a wrestling name. The Handy Man was one of the good guys, a "face." The others were bad guys, or "heels," and she had names for them too—The Angry Principal, The Curtain Jerker, The Night-Time Visitor.

Uncle Charlie was kind. He'd taken Esther to the drug store on the day Esther had seen the blood in her underwear. She'd found blood there before, but this time it was different, because it had appeared all on its own. Ma said it was Esther's "own fucking problem" and if she was old enough to bleed, well, then she could damn well fix it herself.

Uncle Charlie knew what to ask for at the drugstore, and he told Esther to hide the box in her room for next time.

The Handy Man was out back in his woodshed and Esther walked across the yard to ask him for the bicycle.

"Sure, you can borrow it any time. But first, come inside, girl, I want to talk to you."

Esther stood still. She didn't know if she should go into the woodshed with The Handy Man, even though she liked him.

"Well now, don't be afraid, girl," said The Handy Man, "just come on in here."

As always, Esther did as she was told. She stepped into the woodshed, which was warm and smelt of sawdust and tobacco, just like Uncle Charlie.

"You love Jesus?"

Esther nodded, like she knew she was supposed to, and this seemed to make Uncle Charlie happy.

"Good. You like the wrestling on TV?"

Esther shook her head and looked down at the wood shavings on the dusty floor.

"Me neither. It's fake, you know, all of it. It ain't real, but you gotta admire the theatricality of it. You know that word, *theatricality*?"

Esther thought she did, but she was just a dumb little girl, that's what Ma said. So she stayed quiet.

"It means wrestling is all about *timing*. Timing, and *winning the crowd*. Me, I likes fishing. Fishing is about patience and perseverance. You run along to the store now, or there'll be a hiding waiting on you from Ma."

There was always a hiding waiting from someone. Esther started thinking about Jesus. She heard The Baptist Preacher saying, "Jesus Saves! Christ is your saviour!" But Christ was no saviour for Esther. She thought about the wrestler on the canvas—face contorted in pain and suffering—trapped in a *figure-four leg lock* or a *Boston Crab*. All he had to do was submit. Just tap out and it'd all be over, the bell would ring, and the fight would end. But Esther couldn't tap out. For her, there was no bell and there was no saviour.

She thought about the words Uncle Charlie had said to her as she rode the bicycle to the store. At first, they didn't seem to make a whole lot of sense.

Patience and perseverance. Esther got the smokes and the liquor from the store and when she got back to the house, she took the *elbow-drops* and the *flying-knees* and the *stink-faces* and the *full nelsons*, and she let Ma call her "a dumb little whore" when she found the box in her room.

Winning the crowd. Esther smiled and told The Angry Principal that she'd just gone and blackened her own eye, that she was always so clumsy, even though it was Ma who'd bounced her head repeatedly off the turnbuckle.

She smiled at Ma through all of it, and she choked down Ma's rancid cat-shit eggs on Sundays.

Timing. She waited under bedsprings and kitchen tables, learned to play possum. Then, one afternoon when the boys were out in the yard and Ma was asleep in her armchair, Esther took her chance. She tiptoed out from the shadows and snuck up behind old Ma. The one wrestling move she had learned best was the *sleeper hold*, and she clamped it down on Ma's neck before she even woke up, gripping on tight for all her life.

Esther knew that wrestling was fake, but there was nothing fake about the way Ma's legs kicked and spasmed as Esther held on to her neck. There was nothing more real than the way Ma gurgled and drooled as Esther crushed the breath right out of her jerking body. Ma scratched at Esther's forearms, tearing away strips of red-raw flesh. But Esther didn't feel the pain of it, for she'd learnt to feel nothing at all.

Esther rolled back, exhausted, onto the canvas. She reached up from the mat and tagged her partner Arnold into the match, pulling herself up on the ropes. And to the roar of a thunderous crowd, the two victors left the arena as the bell finally rang, Esther The Shadow Girl and Arnold The Protector, riding away on Uncle Charlie's bicycle.

He did say she could borrow it any time, and she hoped he wouldn't miss it too badly.

THE CLAMPDOWN

"Your attitude, not your aptitude, will determine your altitude."

- *Zig Ziglar*

"They put up a poster saying we earn more than you, we're working for the clampdown."

- *The Clash*

I turn down the radio in my car—talk radio—some crappy awful phone-in show providing a platform for the permanently incensed, middle-aged, middle-class, pork-based white man to share his righteous views, dressing it up as 'debate' for my amusement and I insert a CD album (yes my car is that old), 'London Calling' by the Clash.

I chew the last remaining bite of my egg McMuffin, stuffing the greasy wrapper into the cup holder and, as I pull into the carpark of MiComm HQ—my place of work, I skip to track 9 'Clampdown' and turn the volume way up.

"Taking off his turban they said is this man a Jew? They're working for the clampdown." Joe Strummer spits out the lyrics with classic punk vitriol over a pounding backbeat. I sing along, through mouthfuls of egg.

I've turned it up in the hope that someone (preferably female) will hear the track blaring out of my crummy VW and they'll think that I, Steven Edward Anderson, am pretty fucking rock and roll (compared to most Regional Telephony Systems Sales Representatives, that is).

Wow, she will think, *Steven is like, way alternative and shit.*

Unfortunately there's no one around to hear The Clash as (for once) I'm actually quite early. So I park up and spend a few moments regarding myself in the rearview mirror. My face begins to melt, my features shift and blur until I'm just staring at two enormous black holes in a formless pink shape. My mouth is a gaping maw leading to a pit of eternal nothingness. *Just a typical Monday morning,* I chuckle to myself, straightening my tie and psyching myself up for another day of corporate Hell.

I am a field-based sales representative. Which means I'm supposed to spend my time in face to face client meetings—driving core efficiencies through understanding key business issues and effective stakeholder engagement. In reality I spend most of my time in motorway service stations or at home (pretending to work) wanking furiously like some deranged zoo animal.

Which is why today I have been summoned for a meeting with my boss Kieron Knox to review my quarterly sales figures which are, by anyone's standards, absolutely shit.

I could very well be getting sacked today but I'm not going down without a fight and like any consistently below-par sales professional, I've got my excuses prepped and ready to go:

1. Unreasonable and unachievable sales targets based on correlation to previous sales figures for MiComm telephony systems sold over last 24 months.
2. Lack of marketing investments and initiatives leading to stagnation within an already saturated marketplace.
3. No man born with a living soul should be working for the clampdown.

I'm supposed to use a keycard to enter the building but I've forgotten it so I push every button on an intercom by the front door simultaneously and Shannon, our receptionist, lets me in.

"Morning Steven," she says in her smily voice. "Bit early for you isn't it?"

Shannon is just so unbearably pretty. In three weeks she's leaving to go backpacking round Australia. I don't think she'll be coming back.

"Yeah," I say with a casual laugh, "I shit the bed again."

Urgh. She doesn't get the 'joke' I'm trying to make. Just crinkles her nose and looks visibly uncomfortable. I take a moment to rain down an apocalyptic loathing upon myself, then I notice what's on her desk.

"Oh my God who put that there?"

Sitting on the reception desk is a toy—a My Little Pony. Turquoise, with rainbow coloured mane and tail. Actually reminds me of Shannon a bit.

"Anthony Burke. Told me not to move it, says he's got more anyway and he's putting them everywhere."

"Big Tone. I'm not surprised."

Tony Burke—top performing salesperson and psychotic office bully, has placed the My Little Pony there as a joke, a cruel one which I and everyone else know is aimed at Benjamin Storey, a shy awkward kid who works in the customer service department.

Young Benji recently let slip some very odd and slightly disturbing information on a drunken team night out. Benjamin is into something called 'Clopping', a particularly niche and confusing fetish which involves getting turned on by pornographic depictions of My Little Ponies. 'Cloppers' or 'Bronies' as they're also known like to create their own material and circulate it online. Unfortunately some of Benjamin's 'work' has now been seen by pretty much all of MiComm's staff.

Obviously, his life is over.

"Poor kid," I say to Shannon, feeling genuine pity for Benjamin.

"I know," she replies, doing an adorable sad face. "As long as you're not hurting anyone then who cares how you get your kicks?"

God I love you Shannon. Marry me and let's move to Australia together even though I don't do well in the heat and I can't surf and I'm scared of spiders.

"See ya later," I say as I slope upstairs to my desk.

I walk past Tony Burke, hunched over a spreadsheet like he's Trump inputting the nuclear codes. He sees me and looks up.

"Did you see it?"

"Yeah I saw it."

"Got loads more. Putting them everywhere. Fucking pervy little weirdo."

"Indeed."

"You got your meeting with Knoxy today haven't you?"

"Uh-huh."

"Hope you put your padded underpants on mate 'cos you're in for a spanking I heard. Knoxy's gonna wear you like a glove."

Big Tone laughs a terrible, sadistic laugh. It echoes round my head as I boot up my laptop and bring up my quarterly sales figures.

Unachievable sales targets, no marketing budget, unachievable sales targets, no marketing budget. In these days of evil Presidentes, working for the clampdown.

I know how Benjamin Storey must be feeling. Actually I've no idea but I have an approximation. When I first started at MiComm I was asked to introduce myself to everyone and (horrifyingly) to tell them an 'interesting fact about myself.'

Foolishly, I told everyone that I used to be in a band. A band called Furious Dad who once put out an EP via a small independent record label and once supported Catfish and the Bottlemen before they made it big. I thought that everyone would be mildly impressed, sort of like, *oh hey that's cool, I play bass if you ever want to jam?*

But. No.

They all thought it was absolutely hilarious. As if the concept of music, and of small groups of people playing it together was every bit as alien to them as clopping.

The whole sales team rushed straight to the nearest PC and googled my band. They played a track off our EP entitled, 'Disappointing Avocado.'

"*Disappointing Avocado, the kind you never want to eat / Disappointing Avocado, the colour, of your mother's, bathroom suite / In the 1970's ...*"

I sung it in a kind of Morrissey-esque drawl. It was meant to be slightly ironic, off-kilter.

They all laughed as if it were the funniest thing they'd ever heard but the thing was: they didn't think they were laughing *at* me. They thought they were laughing *with* me because they assumed that I thought it was hilarious too.

They were convinced that having reached this point in my life, five years after the break-up of my band and now working in a sales job at MiComm, I should be able to look back at Furious Dad through 20/20 hindsight and see the funny side, see just how much of a joke we were, like someone looking at a photo of themselves wearing a shell-suit in the nineties. Only they didn't realise that I loved that shell-suit more than anything else in the world and still do. That shell-suit, was who I was.

In the aftermath of this episode, I learned to keep my head down, to assimilate. There's just one tiny part of me left that secretly hopes someone hears The Clash blasting out of my VW, if only for a second. Because that's as rock and roll as I'm ever going to get.

"Mr Anderson." Jumping Jesus on a pogo stick that's Knoxy! He's crept up behind me like some sort of horrible ninja. He always says my name in the voice of Agent Smith from The Matrix, as though it's a recent cultural reference like 'How you doin'?' or 'Wassssuuuup!'

I laugh. A high, startled laugh. I always do whenever he does the Agent Smith voice, it's fucking hardwired into me like some demented Pavlovian response mechanism.

Kieron Knox—Mr. MiComm. Destroyed every sales record in existence before being promoted to Sales Manager and then Director of Sales and Marketing. Shaved head, thick-rimmed glasses, navy blue suit with club stripe tie, done up in an offensively large, double Windsor knot. I am literally trembling before him.

And I looked, and behold, a pale horse! And its rider's name was Death.

You start wearing blue and brown and working for the clampdown.

"Are you ready for a chat mate?" Knoxy asks. In the same way a man might ask, *'Are you ready to have your spleen removed violently through your ears?'*

"Yes I think so."

"Good, I've booked a meeting room. You fancy a coffee?" This means he wants me to make him a coffee.

"Sure, I'll just nip to the kitchen and meet you down there. What would you like?"

"Just a black coffee please mate. No milk."

Sweet Jesus how has it come to this? Taking orders from a man who feels the need to caveat a request for a *black* coffee. Does he think I'm too stupid to make it? I've been to University for fuck's sake. Maybe I should just get a job as a rent boy and be done with it? It's basically the same as what I do now and at least I'd have an easier time looking myself in the face every morning.I make two coffees and take them to a small, windowless office where Knoxy sits at a desk with his laptop and leather-bound notebook. Ready to interrogate me and ruthlessly dissect my failures one by one.

"Have a seat mate." I immediately obey. I would've jumped onto his lap if he'd told me to. "Now I just want to go over your performance for this quarter, obviously we're still quite a way below where we need to be."

"Well, the thing is …" I feebly reply, "I've been thinking and well … I feel that my targets are quite high and with no marketing budget they don't really correlate to what …"

"Let me just stop you there mate."

"Ok."

"Because what I'm hearing is The Tiger."

What fresh hell? "I'm sorry?"

"The Tiger. The Tiger is everything that you're afraid of, everything stopping you from reaching your full potential, achieving your goals. Look, your targets are your targets, I can't change those." *He definitely could.* "And never mind what Marketing are up to either." *He is the head of marketing.* "This is about you and how you're going to tame that Tiger."

"Ok." Is all I can think of to say. I was not expecting this. "I mean … I suppose it is the Tiger, but then again, maybe there are some other external factors …"

"It's the Tiger."

"Yes. I see that now." *That's it, he's broken me. For the wages of sin is death …*

"Good boy. Now look, I know you're struggling, maybe that's my fault for not giving you enough of my time, so from now on I want you in the office early, every day, with me. You and I are going to cold-call our fucking nuts off ok? Just sit down with a fucking phone book and call and call and call until we've gone through the whole fucking thing and then you know what? We're gonna start again." *Kill me now.* "Then you're gonna smash your sales targets out the park next quarter and I'll take the whole team out for beers. Fuck it I'll even take you to the strip club and you can see some tits for the first time in your life how does that sound?"

It sounds like a terrible waking nightmare from which there can be no escape. "It sounds … .great."

"Good lad. We'll start today. Get back up to your desk I'll see you there in fifteen."

I do as I'm told. As I walk out the room and back upstairs to my desk, I feel like a death row prisoner whose execution has been cancelled at the last minute. Only now I have to go back to my cell for the next thirty years.

Knoxy is certain I will comply because (and he knows this) deep down, I want to please him.

You grow up and you calm down and start working for the clampdown.

I slump down in my seat. Consider going to the kitchen and making another coffee. Or going to sit in a toilet cubicle to cry for an hour.

As I bring up my inbox I see an email from Shannon with the subject line, 'Clopping NSFW'. It's a link to Benjamin Storey's Tumblr page and the content is … staggering.

The images, on face value, are pretty horrifying. It's not just that it's weird to see My Little Ponies engaged in all manner of acts with freakishly oversized genitalia and sex toys. It's also the infantilised nature of the whole thing which is deeply unsettling. Benjamin is a bit of a perve, that is for sure. Certainly a fucking idiot for mentioning this to anyone in the first place but, as I stare at the brightly coloured sexual equine cartoon content on the screen before me, I can see he's put a great deal of time, effort and even (dare I say it?) *love* into these. The very fact they even exist demonstrates he has a passion for creating them and to actually share them with other internet-dwelling ghouls who're all probably crippled by loneliness in the real world but who, for all I know, get a tiny bit of solace from something they all enjoy together. The fucking band of weirdos.

I find it difficult to tear my eyes away from what I'm seeing. He's definitely captured something. I'm not quite sure what it is. But it's something.

LUXEMBOURG

Julia returned home from her business trip with the small state of Luxembourg in her purse. Her husband, Mike, knew something was up right away and wasted no time in confronting her over his homemade moussaka that evening.

"You've done it again haven't you?"

"What?"

"You know what."

"No."

"Don't lie to me Julia, it's written all over your face. The lying is worse than the stealing."

"Liberating."

"It's *stealing* Julia." Mike slammed his fist on the table with just enough force to tinkle his cutlery but not spill his Malbec.

"It's only a small one," Julia said, flashing her best puppy dog eyes. "Barely even a country really. It's a Principality, I think."

"No it's not. It's a Grand Duchy. You're thinking of Monaco, the last one you got caught with."

"What's the difference? Both ruled by some silly man in a hat."

"Well, a Principality ... wait. I'm not having this conversation. Tomorrow you're taking Luxembourg back and you're going to apologise and hope they don't throw the fucking book at you! Then we're making you an appointment with Doctor Frobisher.

It's time to grow up, Julia." Mike stood up to leave the table, flinging his napkin down for gravitas.

"Where are you going?"

"Bed."

"You haven't even finished your supper."

"I made that moussaka for you! Because I was excited to have you home. It's spoiled now."

Alone in the candlelit kitchen, Julia opened her purse to gaze at her newly-pilfered dominion– all the little Luxembourgians going about their business, completely oblivious to having been stolen.

"A Grand Duchy," she whispered.

She plucked a lash from each of her eyelids, dropped them down into the purse, so that they might fall like tar-black feathers and land on an old lady's shoulder, or a young mother's new dress. They would look up at the sky, strangely different today, and think that somewhere just out of sight, a covetous crow was watching them.

With nothing else to do, Julia headed to bed. In the bathroom, haloed in the light of the vanity mirror (the his and hers sinks—a "must have" she'd informed the interior designer) she brushed her teeth with her electric toothbrush, the pressure sufficient to lift the day's buttery film without disturbing the little crocus flowers of her molars. She removed her makeup, wiping away the layers to reveal the subtle landscape of the years that had passed. The slow undulations of time that could never be rolled back. Some nights she longed for when there was just one sink, and they always left their toothbrushes touching in the glass.

As she lay in bed, beside the pale slab of her husband's back, it was only the thought of Luxembourg, sleeping soundly beneath its silken firmament, that would sustain her through the long night ahead. She was dreading taking it back, and knew how dearly she would miss it.

Mike, a light sleeper, and never one to hold a grudge, turned to Julia and offered her his arm, which she folded gratefully around herself.

"I know why you do it, you know," Mike said. "Luxembourg, Monaco, Bermuda, all the rest of them. It's for tax purposes isn't it? I keep telling you Julia we're doing fine. Just let me worry about the finances, you work hard enough as it is."

"Ok." Julia said.

"And listen, fuck Doctor Frobisher, just take it back within twenty-four hours, ok?"

Mike was a good man, and theirs was a good life. He always cooked dinner when she came home from a business trip, and without hesitation he would place himself at the centre of an international diplomatic incident, right there by her side.

Men always needed a reason for things. But Julia could never explain the feeling it gave her, to walk around with a whole country, snug inside her purse—a secret, known only to her. All those lives stretching off in every direction, infinite possibilities to be nurtured like a candle's flame.

And how could he know? For she had never told him—about the test, the two pink lines, the little ball of cells and how it all came to an end, alone on the bathroom floor.

Sometimes these things just happened, that's what she was told, and she'd learned to live with the truth, in her own way. You could do everything you were supposed to, make the perfect home—safe and warm and lovely. And sometimes, for no reason at all, the tiny little people you put there, simply weren't meant to stay.

YOU'LL NEVER BE A CAT

"Tell me why you're here," said the doctor, from behind half moon spectacles and a jackdaw fringe.

Tabitha shifted uncomfortably in her chair. She didn't know how to answer, and her only thought was *I thought you got to lie on a couch when you came to therapy?*

"My mum told me to come," Tabitha replied.

Opening her leather-bound notebook and unscrewing the cap of her gold fountain pen, the doctor exhaled like a deflating balloon. Pressing on, for time (she assumed) was finite, she asked Tabitha, "Why do you think that was?"

There was a couch in the office (Tabitha had her eye on it) an expensive looking chaise-longe finished in cream-coloured brushed velvet. A beam of late afternoon sunshine was slanting through the window onto it, creating the perfect, warm patch for a snooze.

"For a while," Tabitha began, "I've felt ... different." She spoke slowly, with difficulty. Labouring through the words as though they were bricks she needed to move. "I'm not what I'm supposed to be. I'm not human. I'm a cat."

The doctor pushed her spectacles up over the slender bridge of her nose and leaned forward quizzically, like a heron on a riverbank, "Tell me more about that."

Tabitha didn't know how to express herself any more succinctly than she already had. She felt that to try and do so would be futile—and she knew how this went—you had to give them something they could grasp, if only to reassure them they had all the answers. So she decided to fall back on an old staple and said simply, "I don't fit in."

"Hmm," said the doctor, scratching four words into the page of her notebook with her gold fountain pen.

Tabitha felt a powerful urge to strike the doctor, to paw-slap the glasses off her stupid birdy face. She didn't want to be here, but she knew you had to talk or they would come for you—belt you down, wire you up. Light you up like fucking Christmas to make you sing, sing with the choir damn you! Frenzied and exultant you will prostrate yourself before us. It's for your own good, child, this was all explained!

There was a paper weight on the doctor's desk—spherical, pink and white marble. Tabitha reached out her hand and rolled it gently with her fingertips.

"Please don't touch that," the doctor said.

Tabitha's eyes narrowed, and she stared at the doctor as she moved the paperwight slowly towards the edge of the desk.

"I said don't touch that."

With a final, laconic *swish*, Tabitha pushed the paperweight to the floor. As the doctor stood to retrieve it, Tabitha hissed in her face, startling the doctor, who drew her hand to her chest, and stared—wide-eyed and open-mouthed in disbelief, as the shy, young girl in her office bolted from her chair, straight out the open window.

Outside it was blessed sweet night time. Tabitha jumped down from the fire escape to the cobbled street below. She looked up at the starry sky and screeched her curses up at the Moon. The Moon was Robert Smith from The Cure, he's been doing both jobs since the late eighties. Don't call it "moonlighting", he doesn't like that joke.[1]

1 Robert Smith definitely does like that joke. He thinks it's hilarious but he's not telling you that, stupid, he has an image to maintain.

Robert Smith took the curse and put it in a satchel. Then he rolled off across the sky to go and fire the curse at two lazy lovers, sleeping sound and smugly. Don't misunderstand, the Moon's not wicked, but people only want to hear the *Greatest Hits* these days and there's still so much misery to go round. Call it a creative outlet.

Feeling lighter, spritelier, spry and nimble, Tabitha ran for the fields. She clattered and skittered across glassy, frozen ponds, collecting bullfrog stares. She chased rabbits and hares and weasels down twisted burrows and emerged through tangled roots into a dream-lit meadow.

She found her friend Mr Scarecrow and the two of them danced a quickstep on top of pointed wheat-ears while Robert Smith boogied across the sky singing, *"hand in hand is the only way to land, and always the right way round ... "* Yes it's an obvious choice, but everyone gets one Greatest Hit per month, and Robert is fond of Tabitha.[2]

After the dance has ended, Tabitha returns, as she does every night, to sit silently and still on a bench in the churchyard until dawn, her delicate head resting on featherlight paws, ears pricked, eyes closed ... but watching. She convenes with astral planes, moving softly down starlit corridors, trying to find the one who went away, the one she misses as though she is a part of her, the one she will never stop searching for.[3]

Tabitha purrs and sings to herself, *"hand in hand is the only way to land, and always the right way round, not broken in pieces like hated little meeces, how could we miss someone as dumb as this?"*

When the church clock strikes morning, Tabitha winds it back.

Now she is back in the doctor's office, pondering the question asked at the start, "Tell me why you're here?"

"My mum," she replies, and the words feel lighter—two little kites on a breeze.

---

2 The song *The Love Cats* by The Cure is actually one of the main reasons Tabitha decided to become a cat. It's so wonderfully, wonderfully pretty.

3 If you ever find yourself lost between astral planes, give your eyes time to adjust. You may find that what you thought was just black sky and stars, is actually many pairs of cat eyes watching you. Stop and ask for directions, they may give you a bit of sass, but they're generally pretty helpful.

"I know sweetheart," says the doctor, with a kind smile. She looks down at the four words written earlier in her notebook:

Complex Bereavement Disorder—Mother.

And somewhere in the gardens made of nighttime, a scarecrow puts his headphones on. He doesn't hear the scratch of vinyl, as "Disintegration" starts to play.

DOG FACE MALONE, MEET LINDA

I'm in a hospital waiting room, squinting against the violent iridescence of a thirty-thousand watt strip-light which illuminates this purgatory and sears itself into my hungover brain. The walls are a Hellish beige and there's the usual accoutrements—uncomfortable plastic chairs, out of date magazines, slumping elderly people and a strange sort of play area designed to amuse small children, arranged there by people who presumably have never had (or indeed been) a child.

I approach the reception desk.

"Name?" The stoically unwelcoming receptionist asks, without actually deigning to look up.

"David Bainbridge," I sigh, before adding, forthrightly, as if it's an achievement to be proud of, "I've got an appointment."

The receptionist looks up at this, probably wondering, as I am now, whether anyone has ever strolled into the oncology department purely on a random impulse.

"Ah yes, Mr Bainbridge. Your appointment was actually at ten-fifteen so we'll have to see if the consultant is prepared to see you."

It is ten twenty-two am. I have been here more times than I care to count and have never had to wait less than thirty minutes past my appointment time but clearly, I am holding them up.

"I see. And how long will I have to wait for a decision?"

"Just take a seat."

"Very well."

I sit down. There's a woman opposite me, early forties probably, quite attractive. A child, presumably her progeny, is sitting on the floor at her feet, playing with an abacus.

She glances furtively at me with a pained expression. It looks as though there's something terrible happening to her—death, most likely—but the look on her face, it's something else."How old?" I ask, snatching at any question I can in order to validate the awkward fact our eyes have just met.

"Sorry?" she replies, immediately on high alert to the slightly creepy man who's just started interrogating her in the oncology waiting room.

"I mean the kid," I say, trying (failing) to put her at ease. "The little chap. They're lovely at that age aren't they?" (what age?) "Then they grow up of course."

She winces slightly, visibly recoils and turns away to ensure she can't accidentally make eye contact again. The expression on her face is more than pain. It's the look of someone trapped beneath an unbearable burden. I recognise it—it's guilt. What's she got to feel bad about? Why do we all feel the need to apologise for our own mortality? Like we haven't done enough, tried hard enough. Like we haven't earned the right to bring the curtain down without giving the ungrateful crowd an encore.

None of this is doing anything to mitigate the effects of my hangover.

Last night was a family dinner, in as much as the term "family" applies to our situation. Me, my ex-wife Helen, an interloper and pendulous ball-bag of a man who she calls her husband, Iain. And my son and daughter, who have recently transitioned from actively despising me into a rather cold state of indifference.

I had planned on introducing them to Linda but there's just never a good time and last night would've been out of the question.

Halfway through the meal, just as I was wondering why on earth I'd been summoned to a vegan restaurant on a Tuesday night, Rebecca my eldest, announces she's getting married. Her fiancé Richard, an irksome little toad who has never shown me even a modicum of respect was not present at the meal which made me think this news was not, in fact, new. This was all just for show—something they'd tacked on so at least they could say they'd done more than just send me a text. They'd long since toasted with champagne and nibbles. Ex-wife Helen and super step-dad Iain, headstrong daughter Rebecca and wayward stoner son Jamie, all congregated around the centre island in a bright and warm kitchen which used to be mine.

I told them all I was "delighted" and politely enquired as to where Richard was and why he couldn't face me, to which I received no response. The only thing going through my mind was *how am I ever going to introduce them to Linda now?*

So I just decided to get drunk. I have a horrible memory of berating the poor, bewildered waiter for not knowing what a martini was. Then snapping at him to just "bring me a glass of the coldest white wine you have, as long as it's not Chardonnay." I tried to order a steak, proclaiming that since all normal restaurants offer at least one vegan option, they were in fact discriminating against me as a carnivore. My memory is hazy and I think it all ended badly. I have a very bad feeling I left a voicemail on Helen's phone ... but what?

"Mr Bainbridge?" the receptionist's voice slaps me out of my profitless reverie. "Doctor Qureshi will see you now."

"How kind," I say, standing up and striding from the waiting room, weighing up the idea of ruffling the kid's hair as I walk by but deciding against it.

Inside Doctor Qureshi's office he greets me with his warmly sombre expression and extends to me his soft, dry, brown hand. His fingernails are always rather disturbingly long, although meticulously clean and trimmed.

"Mr Bainbridge, please take a seat. How are you?"

"Fine I suppose."

"Any nausea, dizziness, shortness of breath since we last met?"

"Yes, although I think that's just the cheap Chardonnay which was forced on me last night."

Jokes. Always the jokes.

"I see. Well look I'll come straight to the point, we've had the results back and the tumour ..."

"Call her Linda."

"I'm sorry?"

"She has a name. Please address her as Linda."

He looks worried. I'm sure if he had some sort of emergency button under his desk with which to summon a gang of battle-hardened orderlies armed with sedatives and a straitjacket, then he would be discreetly hammering it right now.

"Ok ... Linda has slightly increased in size. It ... *she* is still what we would describe as a peripheral carcinoma and there don't appear to be any metastases present. I would strongly recommend that we discuss treatment options with a view to proceeding without delay."

I consider this for a second. It's basically the news I was expecting, and I'm prepared for it. All of this has gone on long enough. I've been convinced for a long time that the Universe will let me know when it's time to check out. I'm amazed it's taken this long.

"Let me tell you a story doctor." His eyes plead with me not to, but I continue nevertheless.

"When I was about ten years old, my elder brother, Timothy told me about a man who lived in our town who died in a car crash. I don't recall any of the specific details except that when the crash happened he had his dog in the car with him. I think when Timothy told me the story it was a Jack Russell or something but anyway, the crash was a bad one. So bad in fact that both man and dog were completely pulverised by the impact. When the ambulance came to literally scrape them off the road they had no way of telling which bits were the driver and which were the Jack Russell, so they just shoved them all into the same bag together. There was nothing else they could do. So the story goes that the driver came back as a ghost—half man and half dog. Some sort of grotesque amalgamation of both creatures all bloody and torn up from the crash. Ribcage exposed, guts all hanging out, body and head of a man but with doggy facial features so—big ears, tufts of hair and whiskers, a wet nose and of course a big slobbery dog-tongue and sharp, pointed teeth. Timothy told me to watch out because when I was asleep at night Dog-Face Malone was going to creep into my room and wake me up by licking and slavering all over my face. Then he'd start to bite and scratch at me, trying to tear me up just like him. It was absolutely terrifying to be honest but you see where I'm going with this?"

"No."

"Nothing is ever really created or destroyed doctor. Matter can only ever be transferred from one form to another. The law of conservation of mass. Nothing is permanent you see. Not you, not me and not anything in this world. Everything is transient. We're all just random collections of atoms floating around in space and sooner or later we all end up as a load of dog and human parts all smooshed up together in a big bag."

"Mr Bainbridge it's perfectly normal in your position to feel overwhelmed. If you like I can refer you to ..."

"No thanks doctor. I appreciate it, I really do, but that's it for me."

"May I suggest you take some time to think about your treatment options?"

"You can think about your options all you like. I'm off. Maybe that doesn't fit with your perfectly ordered view of the Universe. Beads all neatly aligned on the abacus but I embrace the chaos because baby, I'm an anarchist."

And with that I head for the door of the good doctor's office. Straight out into the void.

"Mr Bainbridge?" I stop at the door but I don't turn around.

"What is it doctor?"

"You left your coat on the back of the chair."

"Oh. Thanks I do need that, it's rather chilly outside, unseasonably so for this time of year." I pick it up then walk back out into the (rather chilly) void.

Later that night I've had a bit to drink, rather a lot actually, truth be told. I thought I knew exactly where I was going with this. I thought Linda and I had forged a tacit agreement, that our destinies were intrinsically linked and we would walk, hand-in-hand, into the sunset. Now it's more like I'm wandering around in the gloaming, lost and alone. Trapped in the woods.

It's this wedding business that's thrown me. A man is supposed to walk his daughter down the aisle. Supposedly it's what every father dreams of. Trouble is, it's her moment, not mine.

When Helen and I split, I still thought of myself as a young man. I believed there was a second act for me to play. A part of me even felt I was owed it—for all the dreary Saturdays spent at the park when we used to be out to lunch, sipping cold white wine. For all the hours I had to work to pay for nurseries, private schools, riding lessons, football boots. Every Sunday morning I stood on the sidelines watching football matches with Jamie an unused substitute. Trying to encourage him, even though he reminded me so viscerally of myself. I hated having to watch him fail.

I moved away, started new relationships, all doomed of course—women closer to Rebecca's age than mine. Every fucking cliché in the book. I embarrassed my children, and looking back I can see why they chose not to be around me.

It's difficult to relate to infants, and teenagers are pre-disposed to be mortified by anything their parents say or do. So you always imagine there will come a time, after their adolescence and before your demise, when everything falls into place. When you finally "get" one another. This should be that time, but it feels so far away. I have no idea who my children are. Their formative years passed in the blink of an eye and now they're bitter, cynical, fucked-up adults with problems of their own to deal with. And worse—while this was all happening, I got old.

"David?" That's Helen. She's come round and is now in the process of tidying my kitchen with the silent intensity of a trained assassin. In her mind there is no problem which cannot be remedied by having a nice, tidy kitchen. Typical Helen.

"What?" I slur back in the same manner as one of our own taciturn teenagers.

"I said, do you want tea?"

"No. I want to be left alone to die."

"Well you obviously don't or you wouldn't have left me that stupid message would you?"

The cry for help. I knew I was drunk the other night but this was bad, even for me. Apparently I'd left Helen a voicemail saying I was going to end it all. Telling her to tell the kids I was sorry, the full works.

"I meant it."

"Well you clearly didn't because it's a day later and here you still are, very much alive and complaining as usual."

"Well it's a good job because you would've been too late to stop me wouldn't you?"

"I'm not good at checking voicemails David. I was in bed when you left it and today I've been playing tennis."

I told Helen all about Linda of course, drunkenly blurted it all out and what does she do? Tidy up and make tea. I could be swinging from a noose or lying in a bathtub full of my own blood and she'd still be rearranging my crockery in the most efficient and space-saving manner. And yet I need her here. She's the only way I can relate to the real world. She's my anchor, my fulcrum, always has been. I know how selfish that is and I realise the message was my way of gaslighting her into coming round tonight, trying to make her feel sorry for me. It clearly hasn't worked in that regard but at least she's here. Because the truth is I've got no one else.

"Now look," Helen begins in her perfectly matter-of-fact way. "About this tumour ..."

"Linda."

"Whatever David, have you had a second opinion? Have you even seen a proper consultant?"

"Yes."

"Who?"

"Doctor Monty."

"Doctor Monty?"

"Monty Ober."

"David that's a French cookery term."

"You're a French cookery term."

"*Monte au beurre* as you very well know, means *to thicken with butter.*"

"You're thick and with butter." I giggle to myself at that one and spill Malbec down my shirt.

"Oh for goodness sake David, come along."

Helen gets a wet cloth from the sink and starts dabbing me with it. She's so close to me and I think about how she doesn't seem to have aged. She's the same as always, slightly bossier perhaps, if that's even possible, but no different. Maybe that's because we've aged together. Travelling in perfect parallel through time as the Universe changes everything around us, except us.

We're aligned.

She looks up at me with those big, grey eyes and I can't help but notice the smooth curvature of her neck. Her eyes meet mine and she holds my gaze for just a second ...

"Stop leering at me David you're making me uncomfortable. Now look. You and I are going to go and see a proper specialist and discuss your treatment options. We're going to get through this sensibly."

"You can do what you like but I'm not going. Baby, I'm an anarchist."

"No you're not. You're a retired financial consultant."

"I'm on a leave of absence."

"An enforced leave of absence, as I understand it."

"Whatever, as usual you have to be right. It makes no difference. We're all just going to end up as atoms all squashed together in a bag like Dog-Face Malone anyway."

"What on earth are you babbling about?"

"Nothing is ever really created or destroyed. We're all just bits of random matter waiting to be reformed into something else so nothing means anything."

"If you say so."

"It's the law of the conversation of maths. I think."

"Not quite, but not far off. And shall I tell you why you know that? You listened to Jamie going on about it at great length at Rebecca's birthday party a couple of years ago, for which you arrived late and behaved terribly but you were there and you obviously do remember it so drop the hopeless nihilist act and start taking some responsibility."

"How dare you." Although she is right. "Clearly you make a point of listening intently to everything and remembering everything and being Mrs-fucking-perfect all the time."

"I didn't say I was interested David, the only reason he wouldn't shut up about it was because he was so incredibly stoned and thought we hadn't noticed."

I do recall the night. The little shit was rambling on about physics and some Carl Sagan passage he'd read, stuffing his face with breadsticks and taramasalata. Eyes bloodshot to heck, reeking of ganja. I don't remember how I felt in that moment—whether I was angry or indifferent, or ashamed or embarrassed. When I think of it now, it just seems really, really funny. I start to laugh, Helen laughs with me.

"He was terrible at hiding it."

"He still is. Now stop wallowing and start facing up to reality please, starting tomorrow, agreed?"

"Yes I suppose so, you are always right, that is of course the foundation upon which our marriage is built."

"We are no longer married."

"Oh we'll always be married. It's like being Wimbledon champion, they can't take it away from you. You're forever a Wimbledon champion."

"Strangely enough David, that might be the nicest thing you've ever said to me."

INFINITE GROWTH

It was a vile morning in Hell. To put it in a context which your mortal brain can comprehend, imagine one of those mornings where you are violently awakened in the pitch black by an alarm that starts with the number five. Outside it is pouring with rain and you've forgotten your umbrella and your train is cancelled. Now imagine all of that again except the alarm is the eternal screaming of the damned, the darkness is eternal, the rain is acid and the train is driven directly into your anus for eternity. And you still have to go to work.

On this particular morning, Baal—one of the seven princes of Hell—commander of sixty-six Hellish legions, was in a particularly fine mood. He was certain today was going to be the day his long-awaited promotion was confirmed. He brushed the teeth and combed the hair of his man head while his two other heads (cat and toad) screeched and chattered in a kind of cheery, demonic chant. He tied his neck tie up in a huge double Windsor knot so it looked as ugly as possible before slipping the tips of his eight spider's legs into freshly polished oxblood brogues (oxblood being the colour of the shoes and also the blood of many oxen, in which the shoes were covered).

There had been whispers, circulating around the water cooler and the impaling-troughs and the trebuchets, whispers which condensed into rumours before solidifying into hard truths. And whatever molecular form they took, they all said the same thing—the old man was taking a step back.

Lucifer had always been a "hands-on" kind of boss. Quite literally. He wasn't really one for the boardroom, preferring to be in the thick of it, on the front line. Elbow-deep in gore and viscera and rending human flesh asunder from sun-up to sun-down. It gave the junior demons a real boost to see Satan himself every day, leading from the front.

But Old Nick was not a young man. And Hell had never been more successful or in-demand. Time was that tempting souls into eternal damnation was all done manually. You actually had to go up to earth and corrupt a priest by fluttering the hem of a young maiden's skirt up over her ankles with a wicked breeze. It was virtuoso stuff, and many still favoured the old ways. But the advent of the digital age had been Hell's most successful project to date. Now, almost every living soul on earth had immediate and unfettered access to the most diabolical aspects of humanity. The seven deadly sins (and countless new ones) had been given the perfect conduit through which to infect the population. And with predictable bovine stupidity, the inhabitants of mortal earth had greedily suckled at the mechanical teat before shuffling, drowsy and bloated, straight into the fiery pit.

Lucifer needed a strategy to cope with the overwhelming influx of souls. But spending all day poring over spreadsheets and performance reports? That just wasn't his style. And besides, he'd worked so hard for millennia, and deserved to kick back and enjoy the fruits of his labour. So Lucifer was to appoint a Chief Operating Officer to manage the day-to-day running of Hell. Zuckerberg was the obvious choice, but his secondment on earth had gone so well there was simply no way they could relocate him now, so Baal was convinced he was next in line.

There was fierce competition of course. Asmodeus was one of the first names that sprang to mind. Demon of Lust and Anger, Asmodeus commanded seventy-two legions of demons (six more than Baal, although Baal's quarterly targets were the same, which really pissed him off). Asmodeus breathed fire and tempted men with his "swine of luxuriousness." There was no doubt he was doing impressive work, plus he was a fucking riot on nights out. That would count in his favour, for sure.

Then there was Paimon, another of the kings of Hell. He gave Baal the creeps—far too tall and sinewy, with a long thin face—like a lamprey with arms and legs. He was always appearing behind you, catching you on Facebook when you were pretending to work. Paimon was a knower of all, and could reveal the mysteries of the earth, wind, water and many secret things. But if you'd ever had to spend two days on one of his training courses then you'd definitely want to decapitate yourself before you'd even had your second coffee. He was a sly fucker, Baal couldn't rule him out.

Baal sat at his desk drinking a soy latte (he was trying a new diet and was dairy free). He used to have his own corner office, with a fully stocked bar and a sofa where he could nap during the day or crash at night after going out on the lash, post-work. But Corporate had insisted on making the whole office "open-plan" which meant anyone could see what you were doing the whole time, it was fucking nightmare. All of the desks were now officially "hot desks" which made no fucking sense whatsoever as they were all on fire to begin with anyway. They'd installed ping-pong tables and beanbags, all to attract a younger workforce who only cared about having a trendy office and had never done an honest day's work in their whole existence.

As soon as Baal was named COO he was going to change it all back to the way it was. Segregation. Hierarchy. Sulphurous lakes of fire. No fucking espresso cart.

He was just going through some of his unread emails (12,789,282) when suddenly his black heart almost restarted in his chest. There it was—a calendar invite from lucifer@hell.com for a 'F2F Catch Up', starting in just fifteen minutes. Baal clicked 'accept', closed down The Daily Mail on his web browser and went to the bathroom to splash some cold water on his face before the meeting.

Lucifer still had an office of course—a beautiful, glass-fronted corner space with Brazilian teak hardwood floors, exposed brickwork, Scandinavian furniture. The boss had great taste. He'd even had a slide installed that went all the way down through the nine circles of Hell.

Baal could see the big guy sitting behind his desk in all his terrible magnificence. He was dressed in a gorgeous, light grey, double-breasted suit, probably from Gieves & Hawkes or Ozwald Boateng. Beautiful silver hair and beard, huge jet-black horns, piercing red eyes behind Oliver Peoples spectacles, by-Christ he was handsome. Baal felt very underdressed by comparison in his boxy and ill-fitting (not to mention blood-stained) suit.

When he got to the door, two figures unexpectedly appeared out of nowhere, fading slowly into view. *What fresh Hell?* Thought Baal. He recognised the first demon as Shax, a Marquis of Hell who was known to be a great liar and also to know whenever a lie was told. He could also remove the sight, hearing and understanding of any conjurer. Shax appeared in the form of a stork and spoke in a soft voice.

"Welcome Baal, please come in," said Shax.

The second demon was Andras. He had the body of a winged angel (completely naked, which seemed unnecessary) and the head of an Owl. Another Marquis of Hell—Andras was known to spread discord and dissension. He was a trouble maker.

These were junior guys—nowhere near Baal's level—so why the fuck were they here? Baal didn't like what he was seeing one bit. He took a seat in front of Lucifer, who sat behind an impressive basket of baked goods and pastries on his desk, flanked on either side by Shax and Andras, the boss barely even looked up to acknowledge Baal.

"So, Baal, thanks for coming in," said Shax in his reedy, irritating voice. "We wanted to address some recent rumours that have been circulating, regarding the appointment of a COO."

Baal leant forward in his chair, his frog tongue darting in and out of its mouth in excitement.

"The rumours are indeed true," Shax continued, "and we wanted to put your mind at rest ..."

"It's not you," Andras cut in.

Baal was stunned. He sat in silence staring directly at Satan who wouldn't meet his eye.

"What the fuck?!" said Baal, absolutely livid that these two hipster suck-ups were telling him what was what. "Who is it then? Asmodeus?"

"It's not Asmodeus," said Shax.

"Paimon then?"

"It's not Paimon either," said Andras.

"We've given it a lot of thought ..." said Lucifer, finally joining the conversation. His voice was like a fine whisky—smoky and warm. "We've decided to offer the position to Dagon."

"DAGON!?" screamed Baal. "THE FUCKING FISH DEMON!?".

"He's not just the fish demon," Lucifer replied, "he's also the baker of Hell."

"The fucking baker!?" Baal could barely even speak now, such was his fury.

"Corporate just felt that a change of direction was needed," said Andras.

"I'll lay waste to Corporate," Baal replied.

"See, this is exactly what we're talking about Baal," Andras continued, making Baal want to smash his patronising Owl face. "You can't just be laying waste to everything all the time. Hell doesn't have infinite resources."

"Yes we do! We're eternal."

"Look ... if you shove a pineapple up a guy's ass, that's great work, no one's denying it. You shove a hundred pineapples up a hundred guy's asses and you're well on your way to meeting quota but you've got to think about the overheads, we have to think about our supply chains. Everything you do impacts our bottom line. Hell needs to do more with less, we've got to start thinking sustainably."

"Fine. I can shove one pineapple through five guys at a time. Job done."

"You're not seeing the big picture. That's operational thinking and what we're looking for is a strategy-led approach. We want to create more value, we need to innovate. You need to get into the mindset that your customer's customer ... is actually *your* customer. Do you see what I'm saying?"

None of Baal's mouths said a word.

"Listen Baal," said Lucifer, "you're a valued member of this team. You've been here from the beginning and of course I count you among my closest friends, but this isn't personal. Dagon, he's doing great work Baal, really innovative stuff. He uses the ground-up bones of the dead for his flour, their blood to warm his yeast and their eyes for decoration. He gathers the knowledge of men from their squished brains and adds it to his baked goods to feed the denizens of Hell. It's farm-to-table, nose-to-tail sustainability. He made these lemon and poppyseed muffins. Just try that Baal, I swear to God it'll change your life."

"Fuck me that's delicious," said Baal, furious at both the fluffy texture of the muffin and at himself for breaking his diet. He threw the muffin at Shax, who dodged it neatly. "You know what?" said Baal. "Fuck all this shit. Someone get Catering on the phone. I'm getting a dirty martini and a bump of Bolivian flake. Who's in?"

"It's nine-thirty in the morning Baal," said Lucifer.

"You've changed man. You never used to care about all this bullshit. You started Hell from the ground down and now you're letting little pissants like these two tell you how to run it. That's not the Lucifer I know."

Lucifer let out a long sigh, two flames licked gently from his nostrils and set fire to a small chunk of his beard. Then he looked at Baal with shimmering, beautiful eyes. "Times change Baal. Times change."

Baal awoke the next morning with a stinking hangover. The kind that feels like your brains are being scooped out with meathooks through your eyes (which in Hell was not uncommon). He'd made a fool of himself yesterday after he got the news. Gone on a massive bender which started in the office. He had vague, terrible memories of making a pass at one of the girls on reception. When she laughed in his face he took it out on one of the work-experience demons, shoving him into a corn thresher screaming, "I AM YOUR SUPERIOR!" He'd had to be removed from the office by Security, and later he'd been ejected from several of Hell's drinking establishments.

There was to be a "Town Hall" meeting at nine am, at which Dagon would be introduced as Hell's new Chief Operating Officer, responsible for all of Hell's day-to-day operations and effectively second-in-command to Lucifer himself. *How had it come to this?* thought Baal. How had he fallen so far from grace?

Baal was running late, and didn't even have time to shower. He arrived at work just as everyone was assembled in the stand-up meeting area. He sidled in at the back, reeking of gin, trying to make himself invisible which sadly was not a power he possessed. The very stench of him was enough to alert everyone to his presence. He saw Lucifer standing on a small plinth in the middle of the office, just getting to the tail end of his speech, "Everyone, it's my pleasure to introduce your new Head of Operations—Dagon!"

Dagon stood on the stage and waved politely to the crowd. He had the head of a fish—a cod or something, Baal didn't know, and on top of his head there was an octopus. The tentacles hung down and gave the appearance of hair.

"Morning everyone, morning. Thank you Satan for those kind words of introduction,' said Dagon, lisping slightly through his blubbery fish lips. 'As many of you know, I have served as Hell's Master Baker for the last two millennia, and so I know first-hand what it takes to run a business focusing on quality and customer satisfaction. I ran the bakery as a boutique business, giving attention to every detail, and I plan to do the same with Hell PLC."

Baal felt as though he was actually going to hurl. The bile was rising up in his throat and he desperately needed to sit down before he fainted. Dagon continued from the plinth—

"In recent times, Hell has been focused purely on acquisition. Recruitment levels are the highest they've ever been, demand on resources has never been greater and the population of Hell is due to grow by at least one hundred and fifty thousand souls a day from now until eternity. This kind of infinite growth is simply not sustainable as a business model, so I am proposing some changes which some of you may find ... slightly radical."

A hush had descended over the meeting space. The demons of Hell were hanging on Dagon's every word. Baal could feel the seismic shift that was taking place in the managerial structure of Hell. He also felt his bowels beginning to shift along with it.

"Hell used to a place for the truly wicked. The real sinners. I'm talking Pol Pot, Genghis Khan, Adolf Hitler, and the punishments used to be bespoke. We used to take the time to truly understand the requirements of each individual we tortured and to provide a service unique to them. Since everything went digital up top and we started doing crazy numbers, we've seen a downshift in quality. That's not your fault. There's only so many demons down here and with so many souls to process we've had to adopt the Amazon approach of "stack 'em high, impale 'em cheaply" when what we really should be doing is taking a more holistic view. We need to work *with* mortal earth. And with God and our colleagues up in Heaven who everyone's forgotten about. We're magical beings. We can use our powers to actually *help* the mortal realm. Climate change, war, poverty, politicians, the cops. We can help fix all of it. Then when life is finally *good* up on earth there'll be fewer people coming to Hell, freeing up resources and allowing us to build a genuinely sustainable business modEURCCHHHHH!!!"

Dagon had stopped talking because a trident had been thrust into the back of his head and out through his fish-mouth. His body now hung limp and lifeless, hoisted on the end of it. The trident was held by none other than the Prince of Darkness, Lucifer himself.

"Woooooooooooooo!!" cried Satan. "I caught me a little fishy! Look at my little fishy on a stick." He started waggling Dagon's body around, poking and prodding at the crowd with the trident as Dagon's corpse flopped wetly from side to side. "I almost let him carry on, he was doing so well. But if you fuckers think any of that is happening then you're even fucking dumber than you look! Baal—we got you good man! You should've seen your face yesterday. Oh man! You got fucking punked, you asshole!"

Ripples of laughter started to emanate from the crowd as slowly everyone realised what had taken place. Satan was well known for his elaborate office pranks. He didn't do them very often, which was partly why they were so effective. Baal was clearly the intended victim of this one right from the start (although Dagon had come off pretty badly). Satan had looked into Baal's heart and seen his one truest and deepest desire: to be a person of consequence. To be respected by his peers and to do work that really mattered, to make a difference.

"Some of you were in on it of course. Shax, Andras—you guys were amazing yesterday, couldn't have done it without you. Baal, you got Satan'd buddy boy. Boooom!!"

Lucifer threw Dagon's fishy body onto the ground and everyone in the room turned to laugh at Baal, who, in a final act of capitulation, soiled himself.

"Now what are you all standing around for?" cried Satan. "Everyone grab a bag of pineapples and get the fuck back to work!"

The crowd gave an almighty cheer, and then began to disperse. Baal couldn't bring himself to go just yet. He stood still, covered in his own excrement. His cheeks—burning with shame and embarrassment —were cooled by a single tear, which cleansed the filth ever-so-briefly from his skin, before evaporating into vapour with a tiny *hiss*.

Baal had spent an aeon in the Underworld, and would be here for an eternity to come. And it was easy to forget, when you'd been in Hell for so long, the Devil could be a real dick sometimes.

NO NON SWIMMERS BEYOND THIS POINT

is what the sign says. So I sit in the shallow end propped up on a floatation device, one of those long polystyrene tubes. I look down at my belly, which years ago I would've been proud to expose in a bikini but now I keep covered by a black one piece "cozzy" as my mother would call it.

I look like a seal.

The water makes the skin on my thighs appear paler. I'm like a cave dwelling salamander, pinkly translucent. They live in total darkness so have "evolved" to the point where they are blind (in actual fact their skin grows over their eyes). They can live for a hundred years.

I consider the salamander's life-cycle, amidst the splashing and the shrieking of my infant son's swimming lesson, and I can't help but think it sounds kind of, nice.

I knew having a baby at thirty-nine meant there was little chance of everything snapping back into place as it seemingly does for women in their twenties, but I was not prepared to feel like an entirely new species of mammal.

Stuart always insists on being in the water with Fletcher during his lessons, I think it's so he can show off to the young swimming instructor with her gorgeous honey-coloured legs. During my pregnancy he was still going to the gym three times a week. After Fletcher was born this indulgence only increased, ensuring he maintained his physique while I was barely even reassembled in the correct order. Frayed at the seams and busted up on the inside—a badly stuffed pillow.

Stuart had his own insecurities about becoming a dad in his forties. He usually has to win at everything but it may affect his bid to become the coach of Fletcher's football team when there's guys twenty years younger lining up to have a go.

I suppose I could forgive him the desire to stay in good physical shape, apart from the fact it annoys me so much that all those gym sessions do seem to have worked. He's never looked better, the piece of shit. Easy to have visible abs when you've not had to spend nine months growing an actual human inside you.

Oh my god how have you never learnt to swim? Is what everyone says, including Stuart's mother, the world's foremost expert on everything. The answer is *quite easily*. It's very difficult to think of a realistic scenario in which swimming against one's will would ever be required. A plane crash in the ocean, maybe.

I always liked to imagine—if that did happen—Stuart could swim me to shore on his back. Now I think he'd be more likely to use my corpse as ballast to save Fletcher, because of course our child is going to win the Olympics and reverse global warming and must be protected at all costs.

Swimming holds absolutely no appeal to me. I've lost count of the number of times Stuart has suggested it would be good for me to "get a hobby" and I give him the benefit of the doubt as I don't think he means it to sound patronising, he genuinely does think an activity outside the immediate demands of motherhood would be good for me and he's not wrong. But why do men always think having a fucking hobby is the answer to everything?

I want to tell him I did have hobbies—wine, adult conversation and not spending Saturday mornings slowly simmering in a poaching liquor of chlorine and child urine bring chief among them.

Fletcher is getting ready to swim five metres across the pool with the other kids. He'll get a badge if he makes it, I'm not sure what will happen if he doesn't.

"Are you ready?" shouts honey-legs.

"Come on Fletch," Stuart roars, just as an excuse to pump his fist and tense his arms.

As the instructor blows her whistle I look down and *Oh good! My legs appear to have fused together.* At first I think I'm turning into a manatee (the gentle sea-cow) but on closer inspection it looks as though they're being bound by a silky material, wrapping itself around them. *Well this is new* I think to myself and to be honest I haven't the energy to complain so I'll just see where it goes.

Fletcher kicks and splutters his way through the water and I wonder if this is what the big net by the side of the pool is for—fishing out drowning children? They'll need to remove me in a minute as whatever it is that's encased my legs is now snaking its way past my waist and up my torso.

But it's fine.

"Come on Fletcher you can do it!" bellows Stuart. *Give it a rest* I think, the poor kid is trying hard enough.

The fine gossamer fabric has now encased my entire body like a sleeping bag, I'm like an Egyptian Mummy. It's pretty cosy in my new designer shroud and no one seems to have noticed, which doesn't surprise me one bit.

The alien fabric covers my head and face, and finally my eyes. Then everything is black, and I feel myself sink beneath the water.

And now something's changed, I've changed. I can feel it. I'm struck with a sudden awareness, like waking up from a deep and dreamless sleep. I poke around inside my cocoon and make an opening, a tiny pinprick of light opens up and I force my newly formed body through it. I see through insect eyes, a binocular field of vision. And when I stretch out and fully extend the spikes on the end of my raptorial fore-legs I realise I am now a Praying Mantis.

I stalk the poolside on bladed limbs, fast and deadly in my arthropod shell. The females of my new species are known for devouring the males after mating and I fix my kaleidoscopic gaze on Stuart, gleefully preparing to bite his fucking head off but then ... I stop.

I wouldn't want to spoil the moment for Fletcher. He's just about to get his first ever swimming badge and I don't want him to have to deal with the memory of his father being decapitated poolside and slowly gorged on by his mother who has just transformed into a vicious, sexually-cannibalistic insect.

So I slink back down into the shallow end and submerge my thorax beneath the cool water. Above the chlorine meniscus, I see my son; Fletcher has nearly made it to the other side, frantically kicking his legs and gasping for breath. There is a look of solemn determination on his pudgy little face as he battles on and I realise he doesn't care about learning to swim, not really, he's just trying to reach his father. Because he so desperately wants to please him, even if it means he drowns.

Fletcher makes it to the other side and Stuart holds him aloft triumphantly. I look down and see my own form has returned to normal. Fletcher is happy in this moment, Stuart too—and I want to be part of it with them. My baby just swam five metres all on his own!

I start to move in their direction, swishing the water away with my hands (thankfully now human again) feeling the way it supports me as I try to get where I'm going. As the floor of the swimming pool drops away, I realise I'm no longer holding my floatation device, the long pink tube. Maybe I devoured it in my insect rage?

Either way, my feet aren't touching the floor and I'm not holding on to anything. And although what I'm doing isn't really swimming (not yet anyway) I'm happy that I'm getting somewhere. Managing to stay afloat.

LYCANTHROPY (WEREWOLF KITCHEN)

Clinical Lycanthropy—a rare psychiatric syndrome in which the patient believes that he is a wolf or some other nonhuman animal.

Jimmy Lupo runs a tiny French bistro out of an old railway arch, tucked away down a cobbled backstreet in darkest Salford. Lit by a single street lamp which illuminates a single outdoor table with a red checkered tablecloth and a sign on the wall that says "Jimmy's".

It's not on any maps, and on dark nights when the fog rolls in off the canal, and the loons and goons and ghouls roam the streets, it's probably not the sort of place you would stumble across.

But those who find the bistro, always remember it. The smell of fresh bread, garlic, confit duck and roast lamb comes wafting from the kitchen onto the street. Steaming pots of bouillabaisse bubble lazily on the stove. Pommes Boulangère are bathed to tender perfection in stock and butter. Jimmy does it all on his own, running the front of house and the kitchen. There are only three tables, plus one out front; you can't book in advance (you can't book at all) so it's sometimes tough to get in. Plus there's always a chance you may get mauled to death or eaten alive, which some diners do find slightly off-putting. Although for most dedicated foodies, dinner at Jimmy Lupo's is something of a badge of honour—akin to eating blowfish sushi. An experience.

Tonight the moon is full and Jimmy expects at least a few intrepid visitors. He's in the kitchen preparing Provençal tomatoes; scooping out the jellied pulp and covering the exposed red flesh with a fine, sandy mixture of breadcrumbs, garlic and parsley—cool earth piled into a freshly dug grave.

This is Jimmy's favourite place, he is calm in his kitchen. It runs on order and precision but through the most primal alchemic processes, it gives birth to beauty, to joy, to life.

A werewolf can struggle to fit into "normal" society. There are creatures on this earth designed to assimilate, to shrink to fit the size and shape of their surroundings. To sit in grey cubicles behind grey desks in equidistant rows. Werewolves do not count themselves among such unfortunates.

When Jimmy tried to hold down a normal nine-to-five he ended up grabbing his boss, Steven, by the tie and smashing his face repeatedly against a desk. The satisfying clatter of teeth on keyboard. He knows he could never go back.

Tonight there is a scent in the air outside Jimmy's kitchen. It floats on the thermals—up above the miasma of ever-baking mulch in the bottom of warm bins, the tang of blood-splatter on cobblestones. Higher than the funk of cheap aftershave and the ambrosial poison of cigarette smoke.

It's a girl.

And not just any girl, this one's hair smells of autumn Sundays, her skin tastes like a freshly-brewed sunrise. Claudia. Unlike most girlfriends who become ex-girlfriends, Claudia was never afforded the catharsis of looking up her ex-boyfriend online. After removing himself entirely from the dog and pony show of social media, there was simply not a trace of Jimmy left as a tangible entity in the (finger quotes) "real world."

Claudia's heard rumours though. Friends of friends of co-workers of relatives of friends, who smugly pat themselves on the back for eating "off the beaten track" have boasted of finding the finest cassoulet this side of Toulouse, before kicking themselves for not keeping it a secret. And any mention of this elusive *maison gastronomique* is usually caveated with a warning of the somewhat menacing Chef Patron who, amusingly, speaks with a thick Lancashire accent. That's how Claudia knows, and tonight she is coming to see for herself, maybe get some of the answers she is owed. And she's brought a date—an American.

Jimmy smells them both before they walk in the door (the American especially) and takes a moment to steady himself before greeting them as though they were just another pair of unwanted customers.

"Good evening," says Jimmy, giving them his best approximation of a smile, mouth contorting awkwardly on one side beneath his beard—like a dog refusing to let go of a stick, or a person who is experiencing a stroke.

Claudia, expecting nothing less than aloofness to the point of indifference from Jimmy, is well prepared to match him in her approach. Calm and polite. Just a girl, standing in front of a boy/werewolf, along with an American she recruited from Tinder as potential cannon-fodder.

"Table for two please," says Claudia, pushing herself up on the balls of her feet as she says the word "two," just as sweet as Jimmy remembers her, piquing his ire even further.

"Right this way," says Jimmy, staring unblinkingly at the obnoxiously tall and handsome American as he guides them the two-and-a-half yards to their table.

"Interesting place you got here buddy," says Claudia's date. "Great, err ... atmosphere." He gestures at the empty restaurant. "Name's Brad."

Of course it is, thinks Jimmy, seating the pair of them at the table farthest from the kitchen in the vain hope the distance might suppress the urge to drown "Brad" in a vat of onion soup.

"I'll be right back to take your order," says Jimmy, somehow managing to make it sound like a threat. Claudia looks up at him and catches his eye with a sad smile—nostalgia? Or just sorry she invited Brad? Either way it's a look which conveys kindness, empathy, friendship. It's a look which is human. Jimmy clenches his jaw so as not to weaken.

"You know what?" says Brad, snapping his menu shut with the authoritative air of a man who is (predictably) about to order on behalf of his date. "Just bring us two French onion soups and two filet mignon. And a bottle of your most expensive wine ... Champagne ... or ... Shat-O nerf durr Pap. Something like that."

Claudia mouths "sorry", while Brad checks his teeth and hair in the reflection of his knife.

Back in the kitchen, Jimmy prepares croutons. Toasting slices of baguette and garnishing with olive oil and sea salt before floating them raft-like in a sea of silky onion broth inside ceramic soup pots. He covers the pots with a mountain of gruyere cheese and places under the grill to melt and char. The soup and cheese should combine at the first intrusion of the spoon, creating a viscous, overflowing ooze. The bowls should be too hot to touch, the soup too hot to eat. The cheese must dangle from the spoon and burn the chins of those eager fools who simply cannot resist diving in. Messy, unabashed, a shared metaphysical experience. So much more than soup.

Claudia knew how to eat, how to enjoy. She liked to try everything. Once said to Jimmy over dinner that she liked opening a second bottle of wine because for a brief while it made you miss the taste of the old one; a feeling you could both share, a sort of 'folie à deux' in microcosm. Such a romantic way of looking at a simple thing. It was hard to believe she wasn't actually French.

Jimmy takes them a bottle of House Burgundy, tells Brad this is what the French drink, he is suitably impressed. He sets the steaming-hot soup bowls down and leans in close enough for the American to smell the sandalwood in Jimmy's beard oil and says, 'be careful.' Claudia tucks in and lets out a long *mmmmmmm* which feels like hot soup in Jimmy's insides.

There are many myths about how werewolves came into being. Some say the first reference came from The Epic of Gilgamesh, where Gilgamesh jilted his lover because she was believed to have turned her previous mate into a wolf. Centuries after The Epic of Gilgamesh was written, this attitude towards women still persists in tabloid newspapers.

Another story goes that Lycaon, son of Pelasgus, served a meal made from the remains of a sacrificial boy to the God, Jupiter. Enraged, Jupiter turned Lycaon and his sons into wolves as punishment.

Vampires are always intrinsically linked to werewolves. According to Slavic traditions, corpses jumped over by a cat or dog automatically became one of the undead. In every interpretation there is a subversion, a corruption of the inherent "godliness" of man which must be punished. It all comes back to religion eventually, of course. Man has sinned and so he is eternally cursed and must repent. But some creatures are even more cursed than men—beasts and demons who have sinned beyond measure, who delight and revel in the drinking of blood, and feast upon flesh.

Jimmy thinks of this now, as he prepares steaks for his two guests, roasting them in the pan with judicious quantities of butter, whole garlic cloves and sprigs of rosemary and thyme. He squeezes them between his thumb and finger to see how they are cooked, still plenty of give, which is how he wants them—red in the middle, not pink. He removes the steaks from the pan and sets them aside to rest, the juices melting back into the meat, relaxing after its ordeal. He deglazes the pan with shallot, green peppercorns and brandy, followed by cream to create a rich sauce. For a garnish, he sautées wild chanterelles and green beans with a little tarragon—the earthy flavours of the forest. And to finish, an unctuous wedge of pommes dauphinoise.

As he looks upon his creation, it occurs to Jimmy that this is all he needs. Fuck the customers. It is the nature of a werewolf to be alone, an outcast living in the shadows.

All things are placed upon this earth to suffer and die. This restaurant that Jimmy loves can never hope to sustain itself. It is already doomed to its fate. It may become popular, then trendy, then tragically hip, eventually passé, and then finally, forgotten. For all things there is a season, until death comes creeping. If Jimmy and Claudia had stayed together, they would inevitably have found a way to destroy one another, for that is the essential nature of humankind.

With this thought weighing heavily on his mind, Jimmy takes the plates out to the only person he ever really loved to cook for, and her date.

As he approaches, he clears his throat and interrupts Brad, who is talking at an offensive volume about cryptocurrency.

"Ribeye cap, chanterelles, sauce au poivre and pommes ..."

"Mmmmph ... oh my god," says Brad, not waiting for Jimmy or Claudia before eating. "This is good buddy. What is this, some sort of creamed potatoes?"

"It's dauphinoise."

"Fuckin' A it's dope! My man!" Brad holds his hand up for a high five and Jimmy's features contort into a snarl. Then there is the sound of a low growl which takes everyone by surprise, including Jimmy. It's followed by the sound of a horn from somewhere outside the back door and Jimmy realises it's his delivery boy, Mackenzie—on his stupid fucking moped.

"Enjoy your entrées," Jimmy says before backing away and going to answer the back door.

Mackenzie is Head of Logistics for Jimmy's main supplier, Fenrir & Sons. He usually shows up on his moped right in the middle of service, not that it really matters but still, Jimmy would appreciate a little bit of notice.

"Alright our kid?" says Mackenzie, when Jimmy opens the door. He's fiddling with the kickstand on his Vespa, getting his foot caught in the bottom of his parka. He's so short he looks like a kid who's borrowed his dad's jacket. His bowl haircut hangs over his eyes, set in place like a blancmange by his helmet, so he has to lean backwards to see Jimmy.

"Good evening Mackenzie," says Jimmy in a low voice, "what have you got for me?"

"Brace of grouse," says Mackenzie, proudly pulling two plump birds from his saddle bag.

"Those are fucking pigeons Mackenzie." Jimmy's lip curls back over his teeth as he eyes the two scabby avian pests.

"Ha! Gotcha! Just my little joke that. I plucked these two plump pluckers out of a fried chicken bucket on me way over here, having a gadabout they were and a gobble, gobble, gobble, oh wait that's turkeys innit?"

"Shut the fuck up Mackenzie I haven't got time for this tonight. I've got ..." Jimmy steels himself to say the word, "customers."

"Ah shite."

"My ex-girlfriend."

"Nah man, no way! Claudia yeah? Shit bro. Listen, this is why you need me. I can be your sous chef." He pronounces the "s" on the end of "sous" because he's had to look it up.

"Mackenzie, even if you were the last chef in Salford I wouldn't hire you."

"Front of house then. Matey D. We need to stick together, same pack like."

"No."

"Listen. Doing any espuma tonight?"

"Oh you remember that word don't you? Yes, as it goes. I had prepared a mussel foam to go with the turbot, which no one ordered."

"Giz a go o' the can."

"Fuck sake."

Jimmy grabs the stainless steel whipped cream canister which he uses to make his foams. The canister has a nozzle and a trigger, and it's powered by attaching a small canister of nitrous oxide to provide the gas necessary to "whip" whatever the canister is filled with.

The youth of Salford have a different use for it though.

"Cheers man." Mackenzie pulls an uninflated balloon from his pocket, attaches it to the end of the nozzle and fills it full of nitrous oxide. Then he inhales the contents of the balloon and holds the breath deep in his lungs. His cheeks puff up and his eyes pop out of his head like a startled blowfish, as the chemical blast-wave hits his brain. Finally, he exhales as his eyes roll back in his skull. "Fuck me man," he says, blinking up at the starlit heavens.

"What is it with you kids and those fucking balloons?" says Jimmy.

"They're ace man. Giz another one."

"No. Now look Mackenzie, stop dicking me about. Have you got my order?"

"Course man, course. Chill your furry boots yeah? Got it right here."

Mackenzie reaches back into his saddle bag and pulls out a fairly small portion of meat, wrapped in beeswax paper.

"Is it fresh?"

"As a fucking daisy, man."

"Not been in the canal like the last lot has it Mackenzie?"

"Nah man, see for yourself."

Jimmy leans in and takes a big sniff. It's good. He snatches the package from Mackenzie.

"I'll pay you at the end of the month."

"Sound man, sound. I'll see you later then our kid." Mackenzie steps a baggy-trousered leg through his moped and gets ready to leave.

"Mackenzie, wait."

"Yeah?"

"I've got some venison heart tartare left over. If you're game?"

"What?"

"I said, if you're *game,* get it?"

"Eh?"

"Do you want some raw venison heart?"

"Sure man, sure. Eh, can't believe you're giving it away, it's a bit dear isn't it?"

"What?"

"See ya later."

And with that, Jimmy sends young Mackenzie on his way, off to make his deliveries to the most discerning clientele in the darkest corners of the Mancunian night.

"Hey buddy!" the sound of Brad's voice pierces the calm like a stake in Jimmy's heart. "This filet is a little underdone my man. I mean ... I asked for it rare but I think this still has a pulse."

"That's how we like it," says Jimmy, emerging once again from the kitchen.

"*We*, meaning ..."

"People. *French people.*"

"Buddy, if you're French then I'm Joan fucking Rivers, ok?

Now listen, I gotta use the john, why don't you introduce that steer to a hot skillet while I'm gone?"

Jimmy grinds his teeth so hard he nearly dislocates his jaw. "Certainly, sir."

"You're a class act my man," says Brad, actually having the temerity to slap Jimmy on the shoulder. "A class act! Now where's the ..."

"It's outside. The moon will light your way."

"THE MOON WILL LIGHT YOUR WAY!" Brad repeats in what he deems to be a "British" accent. "Love this guy babe!"

Jimmy pulls a chef's blowtorch from his back pocket and scorches Brad's steak for a few seconds, leaving it charred and smoking on the plate.

"Well that'll do it!" says Claudia with a giggle.

"Why are you here Claudia?" He regrets it as soon as he's said it. His tone is aggressive, unnecessarily so.

Claudia's big brown eyes glisten, her breath becomes shallow. Her pulse quickens in her neck. "I just wanted to see how you were doing," she says. "I mean, fuck Jimmy you just completely disappeared. Then six months later I hear you've opened your own restaurant. That was something we always talked about doing together."

"We shouldn't be together. We can't. I fear how it will end. I'm not good for you."

"Jimmy, we had one fight, don't be so dramatic."

"It was terrible. I could have killed you."

"You threw a laptop through a wardrobe. It's not that big of a deal."

"The destruction was everywhere. The splinters. The shards."

"It was from IKEA. Second-hand actually. It was always going to break eventually."

"Everything does," says Jimmy. "You shouldn't be around my kind."

"Right. Ok, this really needs to stop."

"What do you mean?"

"You're not a werewolf Jimmy."

"Sssshhh. Keep your voice down."

"Why?"

"Just keep it down, ok. Lest someone should hear."

"Look, I've never seen you turn into a werewolf. Neither has anyone else."

"I nearly murdered my boss. The rage was uncontrollable within me, the lust for blood."

"You mean Steve? He's fine. He plays squash with my sister's fiancé. He quit his job actually, retrained as a teacher."

"Retrained you say?"

"Yes. He's fine. Look Jimmy, I realise you and I, we moved pretty fast. One minute we were just dating and the next we were practically living together and I know that maybe for guys that can seem ... scary."

"What are you suggesting?"

"I'm saying it's amazing the lengths men will go to, to avoid commitment."

"And what about your kind?" Jimmy snaps.

"I'm sorry, my kind?"

"Yes, women." Jimmy makes a sweeping gesture across the room for no apparent reason. "Someone tells you they're a monster ... and you shouldn't be near them. That they'll hurt you in the worst possible ways imaginable and you just assume they're wrong, because you know best. And if you give any consideration whatsoever to the idea they might be telling the truth then you disregard it anyway because you're sure ... completely and utterly convinced ... that you and you alone, can make them change. Can make them be whatever you want them to be."

"You're not a werewolf, Jimmy Lupo," Claudia says, even more vehemently than before. "Steve's fine, I'm fine, my IKEA wardrobe is admittedly fucked. You're a kind and gentle person and the only one who can't see it, is you."

Before Jimmy can react, Brad comes charging back in, slightly unsteady on his feet, obviously a bit of a lightweight.

"Woo! That was a trip. Some homeless looking dude came up to me and asked if he could "bum a fag". I gotta tell you I love the way you Brits talk but I'll be damned if I understand a word of it."

Jimmy returns to his kitchen, shook to his very core. How was it that Claudia didn't see him for the beast he so clearly was? How was it that Steve was totally fine, playing squash? teaching kids? Was Brad even American? Jimmy had once heard the term *solipsism* and vaguely understood what it meant—that only one's own mind is sure to exist. He didn't know that it came from the Latin *solus,* meaning *alone.*

"Hey pal?" Brad yells. "What's on the dessert menu?"

"Tonight we have a pineapple soufflé," Jimmy calls back hoarsely from the kitchen. By now wanting to bury his own face in the deep-fat fryer.

"Two of those chief. Hey babe you know how to tell if a pineapple's ripe? You gotta sniff its butt! Right buddy?" Brad shouts, abandoning all pretext of politeness and switching to full American volume. "You'd know all about that right? Sniffing butts? Awoooo!!!" Brad throws back his head and lets out a howl which he's clearly been holding in all evening.

"Brad!" says Claudia under her breath.

"Ah c'mon babe I'm just having a little fun! The guy doesn't really think he's a werewolf does he?"

"You are correct, Brad," says Jimmy, in a whisper only he can hear. "The butt of the pineapple should smell like pineapple. That's how you know it's ripe."

To break the tension, Brad's phone decides to ring.

"Oh hey babe," says Brad, with no hint of an apology, "this is Carter, my broker in the city, I gotta take this. C- DOG!! YOU MANIAC WHAT IS GOING ON??" He stomps out the door with all the grace and decorum of a baboon at a tea party.

Outside, the October night is cold and still. The air perfumed by the sweet smoke of bonfire leaves. High up in the indigo firmament, two cirrus clouds part like theatre curtains, to reveal the moon in its alabaster glory.

And back down below, Jimmy Lupo steps out into the alleyway, next to the bins. He lights a cigarette (many a chef's guilty pleasure) and takes a deep pull, exhaling a cloud of his own into the moonlit gloom, feeling the familiar tingle rushing through his body ...

There are many words in French cookery which don't quite have a direct equivalent in English *(confit, flambé, mise en place)* These words are the most elegant words—effortlessly distilling the very essence of that which they describe. The French have other such words for existential states of being, feelings we all know but find impossible to describe succinctly. It's a language of great beauty, capable of capturing vast swathes of the human condition in a single phrase.

Jimmy doesn't know the word *manquer* meaning *to lack* or *to be aware that something is missing*. It's where the rather charming *tu me manques* comes from, which means *I miss you* or more literally, *you are missing from me*. It's how Jimmy feels at this very moment, looking up at the moon, acknowledging it with the tiniest of nods, receiving nothing in return.

Inside, Claudia is experiencing this same, unsettling feeling. She doesn't know why, or what has caused it, but she is suddenly very aware that she is alone. As she smells the faintest undertones of cardamom in the baking pineapple soufflés, the hair on the back of her neck starts to rise, as she wonders—what could possibly be taking the American so long?

A BEAUTIFUL PROOF

The girls look as though they're crying, but their makeup stays the same. On the hockey field they flock and gather, a chattering throng of black-winged migratory birds, waiting for the final bell of school to ring. They write messages of everlasting friendship on school shirts, in glitter-stained yearbooks; every sentiment carefully crafted weeks in advance.

Tabitha is the one girl who sits alone on a bench in the schoolyard. She stares down at the empty pages of her yearbook and wonders what the point of all this has been. If five years' worth of Rorschach tests suddenly appeared in these pages she would gain no deeper understanding. And besides, in every ink-splodge, on every page, she would see only one image, one face—Miss Novak.

The first time Miss Novak asked her a question in maths class, Tabitha knew the answer. But when she tried to speak, the air stuck in her throat; her heart hammered against her chest as though it, too, were trapped. The more Tabitha tried to speak, the more the girls laughed. She felt the exothermic reaction of shame, the geometry of anger.

They named her T-T-T-Tabitha, and later, when they'd learned to be crueler, Scabby Tabby. They taught her to stifle her inquisitiveness; to venerate mediocrity; to follow; to un-be.

Miss Novak knew Tabitha didn't want to talk, but did want to listen. In private lessons, in dusty classrooms on sunny days, Miss Novak spoke of complex numbers, proofs and constants. One afternoon she introduced Tabitha to Euler's Identity, how it was considered one of the most perfect expressions of mathematical form. So simple, yet so deeply profound.

$$e^{in} + 1 = 0$$

"We cannot understand what it means," said Miss Novak "but we can prove it, so we know it's the truth. It's such a beautiful equation; they've done studies on mathematicians' brains which show them actually lighting up when they look at it! Right in the frontal cortex, where all your emotions live. I mean really glowing, like a light bulb!" Miss Novak touched Tabitha's forehead as she said this. And though Tabitha didn't really follow the equation, she knew exactly what Miss Novak meant.

On the hockey field, the girls' fake tears have turned to fake laughter. Twinkling xylophone chimes. A well-rehearsed symphony Tabitha will hear forever. To suffer is to learn, and if anyone is leaving here with an education, it is her.

Bright, shiny girls with their ticker-tape smiles. Once they leave these gates they will oxidise and tarnish. Time will dull them. They're already beginning to disperse, marching bovine into some spongiform future.

"Fuck 'em," says a voice behind Tabitha. Of course it is Miss Novak. "You can leave, you know. It's the last day, you don't have to wait for the bell."

But Tabitha waits. She wants to stay here and honour a promise made to herself, that no matter what, she would hear the final bell. It will sound like ambulance sirens, to a girl, struggling to breathe.

JAM

This morning has not been a good morning. The TV started it—the volume turned up to 11, a disgustingly odd number, I could hear its wrongness the second I walked into the kitchen.

Next it was the jam. Raspberry. Hiding behind the hummus and the low-fat yoghurt. A cucumber blocking my access route like one of those giant redwoods fallen across a mountain road at the start of some horror movie. I was distracted, tried to pull the jar out too quickly and dropped it onto the (freshly bleached) floor. I let out a silent howl as the thin glass membrane fell apart in slow motion, the fruity guts escaping in a visceral splatter. While the TV blared away at 11.

And now I'm in the fucking bathroom, crying.

Molly, my daughter wanted the jam because Luke suggested it. She never wants what I offer her for breakfast, which I guess is pretty normal for a three-year-old. So now I'm sat here crying while Luke makes her some white bread toast smothered in the last of the jam that he insisted on salvaging. Sugar and empty carbs, possibly shards of glass. He'll even cut the crusts off for her, he knows it annoys me but he fucking does it anyway so that he can be the hero while I "have one of my meltdowns" in the bathroom.

I sit on the toilet and pee, staring at a cracked bathroom tile which will never be properly white no matter how much I scrub it. When I'm done I stand up and flush the toilet and while it flushes I have to turn round three times on the spot. The end of the last turn has to coincide with the flush cycle completing itself otherwise I need to start again.

I turn on the tap to wash my hands.

As I scrub the back of my left hand I count to three in my head, three times. Then I repeat the process for my right hand. Then it's the same for the palms, the fingers and the wrists. I scrub methodically, making sure the sequence is exact.

The last thing I want is for Molly to see me upset, so I take a moment to compose myself. I walk out, down the narrow hallway of our little flat with the black and white photos of us on the walls—Molly and me—the absence of any men in the photos is at once a source of courage and a stark reminder that I'm on my own.

In every photo we are smiling, laughing. I love to look at them but then I immediately hate myself for thinking that in every one there's a gap, where a man should be. Daniel Fisher, my former university professor (such a fucking cliche it makes me cringe into nothing) is Molly's father. He decided just before Molly was born that he "wasn't ready", said it would be kinder if he wasn't in her life. Then three years later he's got a wife and a baby and pictures on his wall of his perfect family which can only mean it wasn't Molly he couldn't live with, it was me. He sends me a cheque every month. And every month I tell myself I'm not going to cash it but I always do. Who writes fucking cheques anymore? I think he does it to spite me. I could ignore a payment into my bank account, just pretend not to notice it at all, like *Oh My! How did that get there?* But a cheque, requires a physical act, it makes me complicit. Every month when I hand it over at the counter, I might as well be getting down on my fucking knees.

In the kitchen, Luke and Molly are eating their breakfast. Luke is leaning over the table trying to snatch Molly's toast in his mouth like a dog. She screams with laughter—laughter which I feel he is stealing from me.

Luke doesn't officially live with us. He lives with his parents even though he's twenty-five and blames their generation for the fact he can't buy a home of his own. Still lets his mum do his washing though.

Luke is my buffer, my normal. I don't do well on my own, everything starts to close in on me. I abide by a stringent and ever changing set of rules which I impose on myself, one of the most important being that other people can't be allowed to see my 'rituals'. Obviously I can't allow Molly to see me spend fifteen minutes trying to turn the light switch off in the very particular way that just *feels* correct—no one can—they'd drag me off to a secure facility and pump me full of lithium at the drop of a hat. Luke knows I'm an emotional mess and takes every chance to demean me for it. Like most men he gets off on feeling superior. But he has no idea how deep my crazy goes and thankfully his presence in our lives means that I am actually able to leave the house in the morning. When the little voice in my head tells me to throw my keys down a drain for no reason, I'm less likely to do it with him around. All relationships are complicated, and ours works in its own fucked up way.

"Come on guys we've got to go or we'll be late. Molly, don't let that nasty dog eat your toast, you don't know where he's been."

I try to affect an air of cheerfulness. Try to be a part of their fun. Luke is still snapping away and barking. It's actually quite funny. Or rather—I realise it's funny, even though I'm not entertained. These moments are the hardest, when I realise that in spite of myself, I have come to depend on this person who can never really know me and who will eventually leave.

She's becoming hysterical now and I start to panic as I know she's liable to throw a tantrum in the car.

"Luke. Come on we really need to go." He ignores me. "Luke?"

"Yes?" He says, breaking character with an exaggerated sigh.

"We've really got to go or we'll be late and please don't wind her up." I'm trying to say this in a casual offhand way but it's not coming across.

"It's fine we've got loads of time. Let her finish her breakfast at least." He shrugs and turns his back to me, sips his coffee and says, "Molly darling, mummy says it's time to leave so you've got to eat all your toast up now, yeah, for me?"

Molly nods her head and eats her toast like a little angel and once again I am standing here like the overbearing authority.

Finally I get Molly's coat and shoes on her and we're out of the flat, down the stairs, into the cold January air and heading for the car. Luke's catching the bus to work. He'll be back tonight if he feels like it. Otherwise, he'll make some excuse and sit at home in his bedroom playing computer games. I envy him, I really do.

He gives me a kiss before he leaves and says, "Try not to get too anxious today babes. Text me if you need to talk yeah?"

Text you? Because that's what every single mother on the verge of a psychotic episode needs—to have to compose a text message which accurately describes the vast, pitch-black underground cave network of her emotional state, whilst at the same time sounding not *too anxious.* Cheers babes.

It's a short drive to nursery and one I enjoy as long as Molly stays quiet in the back. The morning sun and the crisp frost on the naked tree limbs gives everything a little sparkle. I like winter. Everything stops. Nothing's really dead, it's just suspended in time, waiting to come back to life, taking a moment to be still.

I glance back at Molly in the backseat; her big, wide eyes are taking in the whole world around her. There's no trace of worry and I hope that she's comfortable, comforted. That she feels safe in this moment. That's all I want for her.

We arrive at nursery and I help Molly with her coat. It's a freezing cold razor blade of a day, the kind of day that has clarity. A good day (or at least it would be) if not for the fucking jam.

The smiling nursery school teachers, indefatigably cheerful and full of life, are always there to greet us but it's the hardest part of my day watching her go. Because every time they take my daughter by the hand, I am utterly certain it is the last time I will ever see her. In these moments, all of my most terrible fears are realised at once. I stand rooted to the spot as grainy black and white footage of unspeakable horrors plays on a never ending reel in my head—atomic explosions, tortured animals, infestations of chattering gnawing bugs, skeletal children crying for their mothers. I think of all the things I could've done to stop whatever looming, shapeless nightmare is about to unfurl itself and I know, beyond all doubt, that everything is my fault. I didn't try hard enough. I'm not good enough. I don't deserve her.

IIIIIIIIIIIIIIIIII

When I was little, I thought we had ghosts in our house. I was convinced that things I'd put in certain places were being moved. I used to arrange all of my toys and clothes in very specific ways. Everything had a place. Then I'd find they weren't where I'd left them. My parents laughed it off when I asked them about it but as time went on I became obsessed with the idea that there were people living in our walls who came out at night to steal my things away.

After a while it wasn't just my toys I worried would be stolen, it was my parents as well. I couldn't stop the ghosts in the wall from touching my things. And I couldn't stop them when they decided to steal my dad away. I was thirteen when it happened—cancer—he went quickly. I was convinced it was because of me, because I hadn't tried hard enough to keep him safe.

"Give me a hug to last me till you get back."

That's what he'd say every time I had to leave his hospital bed. I'd give him the biggest hug I could manage, really believing that it would last. He knew of course that it might be the last time I'd see him and then, eventually, it was.

Dad once gave me a little shell which he'd picked up on the beach while we were on holiday in Anglesey. I kept it with me all the time and became fixated with it after he was gone. It was white and very small, perfectly smooth with the faintest residue of salt left behind. When I ran my fingers across it I felt like I was back on that beach with my dad when the sun still shone. Of course I've kept it safe ever since he died, I honestly don't know what I would do if I lost it. I thought that holding onto the shell would give me strength. But as time goes on I find that I can't remember little details about him—the lines of his face, the exact sound of his voice. I don't have the power to keep him with me. And I'm so frightened of losing this object because I know the pain would be too great, like losing him for a second time. The truth is I'm holding onto a relic, something which once protected a living creature but now is just an empty thing. I should have let it wash back into the sea a long time ago.

I think of my life like a Venn diagram; graphs, charts and data have always made sense to me. Numbers cannot lie. Everyone and everything in my Universe has to fit into a bubble. My bubble is the largest, for there is a lot to fit in. Molly's bubble is small, completely enveloped by mine (for now). Luke intersects with both of us which is ok, he only occupies a small sliver of our space. I do everything I can to stay in control of our Universe—I clean, I count, I check. I make sure that everything is balanced and accounted for. The problem is that there are forces outside of our bubble—people and things which are beyond our control and into which we may accidentally bump if we're not careful. People are unstable atoms, an excess of internal energy causes them to become volatile. In order to become stable, they must bond with other atoms. This process can be chaotic, but it must be controlled.

I drive out of town for about thirty minutes, listening to a talk radio station because the inane chatter, the complete banality of it, is like a soothing white noise to me. I stop at a chemist and buy a can of diet coke and a chicken salad sandwich with less than two-hundred calories which I will not eat. I also buy a pair of nail scissors, sealed inside a small plastic pouch. They are only tiny, but I know they are sharp.

I pull into a hotel carpark just before lunchtime, some place just off the motorway with no memorable characteristics whatsoever. Not fancy, but comfortable enough. The sort of place no one would choose to stay for pleasure, only out of necessity. Which suits me fine. This utilitarian stopover seems to exist in nowhere space, a temporary respite in the hinterlands of real life. The reception area is pleasingly beige, there is no one else around as I collect my key card and make my way down a muted corridor to room 48 (thank god we've got a good number or I may well have turned back). A slightly sheepish man answers my knock on the door. Softer round the edges, greyer round the temples.

"Hello Daniel," I say.

Later, after we've had sex in the seedy afternoon dimness of the hotel room, I'm in the bathroom once again. Only this time I am calm.

Daniel is lying in bed on the other side of the door. I left him lying there naked, sheet pulled up to the waist, sparse and wiry chest hair on pale white skin. He's not good looking, not in the same way Luke is, but there is something about him which, to me, feels like home. The sex is ok, fairly pedestrian really, but I like it when he's on top of me, his face goes all serious like he's concentrating hard on some physics equation. Sometimes I feel like laughing but I don't. I please him, I know I do. And when I say that I don't mean it in the same way I please Luke, which frequently involves recreating some misogynistic and degrading act he's seen in porn. I mean *I* please him. Just me.

"Babe are you coming back? I'm lonely here," he calls from the bedroom. I shudder at the the word "babe". It's bad enough when Luke uses it.

"Two minutes," I call back. "Give a girl a chance to freshen up."

Daniel thinks he has made today happen. He'll have felt guilty, messaging me late at night on Facebook, starting off all innocent before furtively engineering this date, deleting the evidence from all devices. He doesn't realise that none of this has happened by chance, it's all been meticulously planned. I knew when I clicked 'like' on his stupid friend's camping photo that he would see it and think of me, just before he was due to travel this way for a conference (his schedule hasn't changed at all).

Daniel doesn't know it, but I'll never let him go. How could I? He's mine and I want to keep him. But only here, in this bubble, where we can both exist together. He doesn't notice any of the ways I pull his strings and when we make love he doesn't notice the six tiny white scars on the inside of my left thigh. One for every one of these hotel room afternoons we've stolen since Molly was born.

I'm making the seventh one now. Delicately drawing the fresh blade of the scissors across my skin, careful not to go too deep. There's a moment when the blade parts the skin, before the blood rushes in—it's like unzipping a dress or making a slit in a ball of dough. When the skin's natural elasticity gives way, there's an elegance to it. I accept the pain, knowing it will come, experiencing the way it floods my body with adrenaline and lights up my central nervous system. In these moments I am floating in ethereal space. I am free.

I apply a thin strip of gauze held in place with surgical tape and repackage the scissors in their plastic wrapper. Then I pull on my robe before going back into the bedroom where the scene is somehow different to when I left it. The colours have been leeched, the volume turned down. I have absorbed them.

Daniel stirs contentedly in the bed, stretches his arms out to me.

"I've got to go."

"What? Oh I thought you could stay for a bit?" His pleading sounds slightly pathetic, his bottom lip juts out in a small pout.

"I'd love to, but I need to get back."

"Well look," he says, suddenly all serious, propping himself upright against the headboard. "Sit down for a second, there's something I need to say."

Shit. *Something I need to say.* This doesn't sound good at all.

"Ok," I say, feeling the first cold waves of panic start to creep up my spine, "say it then."

"I want to start seeing Molly."

The.

Fucking.

Jam.

This is all my fault. How didn't I see this coming?

"What?" I say back, aware that I'm talking but not feeling the word leave my chest.

"I know this might come as a bit of a shock."

"We agreed. It was what you wanted. It was what you said you wanted." I can't breathe.

"I know," he says, looking me right in the eyes, trying to keep me calm. "I know we agreed it was for the best."

"What about your wife?"

"It's complicated. But she knows."

"She knows? What do you mean she fucking knows?"

"She knows everything. She knows about me and you, she knows Molly is my daughter."

"Has she seen her? Has she seen Molly?" My voice is wavering, out of control.

"She's seen your Facebook page, so yes, she's seen Molly."

"I have to leave, I have to go now."

"Angeline." I fucking hate when he uses my full name. "Look I know this is a shock but we can make this work, people do it all the time. I have a right."

"No you don't."

"I know I haven't been a part of her life …"

"And you won't be. She'll never know who you are. You're nothing to her and you're nothing to me."

"I've paid for her!"

Everything slows down. I am filled with a taut, insistent panic, and something much worse—rage. I start getting dressed, fighting my way out of the dressing gown and into my clothes.

"I have to go."

"Look come on, I didn't mean it like that. I just mean I've done right by her all these years. I've looked after you both."

If I was still holding the scissors I would stab him in the fucking neck. He seems to realise this and shrinks under the duvet. Just as he's about to speak he suddenly stares at my leg.

"Fucking hell you're bleeding."

A small patch of dark-red blood has started to bloom on the blue fabric of my jeans, right at the crotch.

"It's fine."

"No, really. I'm sorry but you're bleeding … down there."

I run.

I'm outside.

I'm in my car, driving to get back to Molly and now I'm in a bubble. All of the bad thoughts, all of the worst things that I try so hard to keep on the outside are trying to get in, closing in on me. As I speed along the motorway I'm aware of the thin membrane of glass and metal that is currently the only thing keeping me locked in, locked inside this car. Locked inside my own head. I think of how easy it would be to shatter it to bits, just like the fucking jam. To let all the bad stuff ooze out onto the floor and leave it for someone else to clean up. Make it someone else's mess to worry about.

The blue January sky in my windscreen is peaceful and serene, I can feel myself floating up into it, looking down on myself travelling through space, no longer in one place or another. Apart. Unstable.

I need to get back to Molly.

I need to give her a hug to last her.

I need to let go.

I need to

BEES, MOTHERFUCKER!

Hamsters, guinea-pigs, rabbits—they generally just want to die. Shuffling aimlessly off this mortal coil like lemmings off a cliff. Although nobody keeps pet lemmings, which seems a shame.

Dogs and cats are more resilient. Most of their issues stemming from the fact they're essentially mutants—relentlessly inbred over generations to satisfy the crazed and demented whims of the most godawful species on the planet—us.

Jeff had trained for two years to become a veterinary nurse, and had found out (exactly as advertised) the hours were long and the pay was terrible.

But it was honest. Most of the tasks, while certainly unpleasant, were straightforward enough. The outcomes were self-evident. Office politics were minimal. You knew where you stood with impacted anal glads.

"He's been dragging his bum across the carpet," said the owner of Capers the Cavalier, who was actually kind of handsome (the owner, not the dog). Mid-thirties at a guess, touch of grey at the temples, vintage band t-shirt (Pixies) and thick-rimmed glasses. The type who would have an opinion on which is the best Weezer album (would he lie and say Pinkerton to try and look cool, when really we all know it's Blue?).

"The scooting is usually the first sign the anal glands are troubling him," said Jeff, inserting a lubricated finger into Capers, who didn't make a fuss, though his eyes did bulge slightly.

Jeff had become quite adroit, like an experienced angler tying a fly with a clinch knot, meaning he could study the emo dog owner while he worked—the rectal cavity of the Cavalier King Charles affording him a certain 'cloak of invisibility.'

It was usually easy to tell if the owners were gay. A Pomeranian or a Chihuahua was a decent indicator. Of course there was always a chance the guy was bringing the dog in for his wife or girlfriend. The thing was: the gayer the dog, the greater lengths the straights went to in order to emphasise their straightness. They'd start babbling about weights or football just to try and offset the effects of the miniature Maltese terrier under their arm.

This guy was tricky to get a read on. Although—Capers? Had to be gay.

"The glands are quite full," said Jeff, "but the material is all normal."

Normal. Faecal. Material. There was no getting away from it. Literally. In the first week of the job, Jeff made the error of squatting down at table height to get a better look at what he was doing, only to be hit directly in the face by a sudden expulsion of normal faecal material from the back end of a bloodhound.

He guessed this was pretty much the experience of having children, for most people.

"Sorry, I have to ask," said the owner, "did you used to work at DB's?"

Making conversation, now? Thought Jeff. *Really?* "DB's?" he replied, "the old nightclub in town?"

"Yeah."

"No."

He did. For one summer while he was "taking a break" after finishing his completely pointless university degree, Jeff had moved back in with his parents and taken a bar job at "DB's", the type of dingy nightclub which exists in all provincial towns. The one place that stays open after the pubs shut. Sticky floors, awful music, cheap drinks and random acts of violence.

Surprisingly, he'd quite enjoyed it. For one summer he existed in a kind of hinterland on the outskirts of what normal people insisted on calling "real life".

For Jeff it was the first time he'd let himself go a bit. Most of his life had been spent on the periphery of the fun, viewing it from a safe distance with a wry smile, a casual observer. It wasn't that he was a prude, or a square, or a stick-in-the-mud or whatever the vernacular was. He didn't begrudge other people their fun, he just didn't want to get involved. But why? What higher purpose was he saving himself for? None, he realised, soon after starting work at DB's. He wasn't special. The knowledge was liberating and for once he allowed himself to indulge in a few pleasures—beers at the end of a shift, a singalong to the last tune of the night. A cigarette on the hot curb next to the bins, the night air so thick you could chew it. A snog and fumble in a dark corner.

A good time, if only for one summer.

"There you go Capers," said Jeff, snapping off his rubber gloves and feeding the cavvy a bacon-flavoured treat from a jar. He turned to the owner, who was stroking Capers's head as the dog chomped on his treat.

"He should be absolutely fine, bring him in again if he seems uncomfortable. Anal glands can be a problem for cavvies. The toy breeds have been bred down in size so much while certain organs have stayed close to their original size, so now they're way out of proportion."

"Right. Guess that explains why his nuts are so huge for such a small dog, right?"

Jeff forced himself not to laugh, maintaining a professional demeanour. "Well size is relative I suppose. I wouldn't say they're *huge,* depends on your perspective."

"Right, yeah," said the owner, immediately regretting his comment, the jovial expression sliding off his face. "I mean ... I don't mean compared to ... but, for a dog ... never mind."

"See Kelly on reception on your way out," said Jeff. "Good boy Capers," he added.

And with that it was lunch time. Amazing how the brain learns to compartmentalise what it witnesses in the morning while still allowing one to eat afterwards. Jeff walked into reception where Kelly sat behind the desk. Fresh out of drama school—Kelly's hippie hair and husky voice lent her the perpetual impression of having just returned from a music festival.

"I can't believe he was one of yours!" said Kelly, completely oblivious to old Mrs Tompkins who was waiting in reception with Neville the Shih Tzu.

"What do you mean?"

"Hot indie guy with the Cavalier! He's totally gay, he left you his number."

"He left me his number? Does he want a follow up appointment? We've got his number on the database."

"He wants a follow up appointment all right—but no dogs this time! Strictly "mano-a-mano" if you know what I mean?" Kelly started pushing her tongue into her cheek, moving her hand back and forth with an imaginary grip—the universal mime for oral sex. Then without missing a beat she stopped and said, "You can go through now Mrs Tompkins," with a kind smile at the old lady.

"I'd get in there quick if I was you, son," said Mrs Tompkins as she carried Neville in to see the vet. "Snap him up before somebody else does."

"See!" said Kelly, giving Mrs Tompkins a trigger-finger and a theatrical wink.

"Actually ..." said Jeff, sitting down on the spare seat next to Kelly, "I have met him before. He recognised me from when I used to work at DB's."

"Oh my god," said Kelly, as if she'd just been told the fate of the Ark of the Covenant. "And did you, you know ...?" No mimes this time, it was obvious what she meant.

"No," said Jeff. "Nothing like that."

Kelly looked utterly dejected for a moment, then looked up sharply, one finger aloft, "Hang on," she said. "You met in DB's ...?"

"Sort of."

"And you've got bees?"

"What?"

"You've got bees haven't you? Living in your bathroom? You told me the other day."

It was true, Jeff did indeed have bees. For weeks he'd been noticing a faint, barely audible buzzing sound every time he went into his bathroom. Recently it had become louder, more fervent. What had begun as a single, intermittent buzz had now turned into an ensemble. A choir of bees. He surmised they were living in the bathroom air vent.

He'd looked it up online, and there was no way he could get rid of them. Bees are protected, and in any case they would probably leave after about five to six weeks. Or they would simply burst into the bathroom and assume dominion over Jeff's flat. Either way there was nothing he could do.

"Yes. I've got bees," said Jeff, getting a sense of where this was going.

"You two guys met ... many, many years ago ..."

"Not that many years ago."

"... in DB's. And now you've GOT BEES, and you meet again. It's a sign."

"It's not a sign."

"It's definitely a sign. You have to call this guy Jeff. The universe is telling you to do it. You can't be miserable and lonely your whole life."

"I'm not miserable *or* lonely thank you very much."

Which was true, by Jeff's own estimations he did not feel miserable or lonely.

People were too complicated. You could hold a hamster in your fist—a tiny, wriggling sock puppet—stare deeply into his expressionless face and in that moment, you could get a sense of what he wanted from you, who he needed you to be.

People, blessed with the faculty of speech, were far more difficult to understand.

Jeff imagined his own life as the display on a heart rate monitor. The graph was moving in a regular fashion—slowly up and down—rhythmical bleeps from the machine. There was nothing to alarm it, no stimulus to send the heart rate into a spike, no surge of electrical current to cause any undulations or to disturb the uniform pattern of a life, slowly passing by.

"Look ..." said Jeff finally. "Suppose I do call this guy and we go on a date and it's awful?"

"So what? People go on awful dates Jeff, then they have something to laugh about with their friends, it's called life."

"What if he's married?"

"Ask him straight. Get it out the way."

"Ok, well suppose we have a good date? And we end up getting married and years later we get divorced and hate each other, or he gets crippled in a skiing accident and I have to nurse him and eventually smother him with a pillow out of kindness?"

"You're overthinking it. Trust the bees Jeff!"

"I don't know if I do trust the bees, they aren't necessarily a reliable source of life advice."

"Do it!"

"I'm not sure."

"BEES, MOTHERFUCKER!! Oh Mrs Tompkins, didn't see you there. Take a seat we'll have Neville's medication ready shortly."

Jeff had no reason to believe the bees were cosmic messengers sent to alter the trajectory of his life, but it was something Kelly had said that made him pick up the phone later that evening, after a large gin and tonic had settled his nerves.

... so they have something to laugh about with their friends.

At what point do two people move from being "work buddies" to being actual, real-life friends? This had always been yet another mystery to Jeff, but it didn't matter now—Kelly had made the leap for both of them. And if nothing else came of this phone call then at least Jeff would have something else to talk to his friend about at lunch tomorrow. So he dialled ...

"Hello?"

"Oh, hello is this Mr Spencer? I mean Henry?" *Henry and Jeff*—anyone had to admit that was cute.

"It's Henry yeah, is this ..."

"It's Jeff, from the vets."

"Hi! Great to hear from you, thought you might just go for a text."

"Oh. If it's not a good time I can ..."

"No, no! I didn't mean that ... I mean, I love that you called. Well not *love* ... I'm glad. Glad that you called." Henry's awkwardness was refreshing, and Jeff felt it lifting the weight off of him.

"Well obviously I wanted to check how Capers was doing," said Jeff.

"He's good thanks," Henry replied, seemingly as relieved as Jeff to be over the first hurdle. "He seems more comfortable, he's had his dinner and now he's asleep on the sofa, snoring."

"That's a good sign. Never met a dog named Capers before." Could Capers belong to Henry and Mrs Henry? There was still an outside chance ...

"Capers Nonpareilles. That's his full name."

"What does it mean?"

"Unparalleled Capers."

"Well it definitely suits him. Look, I wasn't sure whether to call, it was my friend Kelly who convinced me I should. And the bees."

"The bees?"

"Yeah, I've got bees. They live in my bathroom."

"Ok."

"It's fine, they'll be gone soon. I've been reading about them—they have one Queen who runs the hive, and her job is to produce eggs until a new Queen emerges and then the failing old Queen is either killed or run out of town by the rest of the hive. She's basically some used-up, faded old starlet whose worth diminishes the older she gets. Then there are the drones—they're all male and their job is simply to mate with the Queen. They're just dumb guys relentlessly trying to fuck but come autumn, once they've served their purpose, they're cast out of the hive. They are literally left out in the cold to die. And the workers, they're all sterile females so of course they're disposable. They have to collect the pollen and the nectar, feed the Queen, clean the hive, make the wax. They even get rid of the dead bodies of the drones. They're the undertakers of the hive! And you know the worst part? Their lifespan is only five to six weeks. One summer. That's all they get."

Silence on the line, apart from the sound of Jeff's own breathing, uncomfortably loud in the receiver.

"Whoah," said Henry after what seemed like eons. "I hesitate to ask but ... is there a point to all this?"

"That's what I've been wondering."

"Is this your way of asking me out?" said Henry.

"Well you left me your number so technically this is *you* asking *me* out."

"Oh, well in that case I'd love to."

Jeff wasn't exactly sure what had happened, and told himself maybe—that was how these things were meant to go. He just had one more thing he needed to ask.

"I've just got one more thing I need to ask ..."

"Ask away."

"What's your favourite Weezer album?"

ERIC THE ASTRONOMER

Eric the Astronomer lives alone, in a tower made of memories. Old notebooks, scribbled front and back. The musings of a day, rendered indecipherable by time. Yellowing sheet music of songs reticently tinkled for loved ones who appreciated the effort. Copper-bottomed frying pans which made French toast on Sunday mornings.

The things that are left behind after a life has happened.

He sleeps most of the day in his bric-a-brac minaret, until night falls and the stars and the planets come out, answering his call to prayer.

With mighty Jupiter he shares a glass of scotch, and talks of his father—of whom he remembers very little—apart from the way he used to wink with just the corner of an eye. How that one tiny gesture would make him feel bigger than himself.

He dances with gentle Venus and tells her his favourite memories of Juliet and the life they shared together. Tonight it's the time it was too rainy to take a boat out on Rydal Water, and a goose chased them along the lakefront. Neptune laughs.

Venus twirls across the firmament, and as she spins, she unravels spacetime like a spool of silk. The fabric of the universe detaches itself, rending apart the threads of this great celestial tapestry, and it's as if Eric could reach out into the nothingness and touch Juliet's fingers one last time.

The solar system rearranges itself around him, and a single object falls slowly from the sky, dragging a comet's tail in its wake. It's an umbrella, and it lands softly at the top of the tower.

And so it goes on for Eric, night after night—this dance, this worship. And every night, Eric's tower grows a little taller, heaven gets a little nearer.

TROY (...OR HOW TO GET TO PENGUIN ISLAND)

It's been eleven months since dawn broke on that awful morning. I had prayed for the night to consume me, to let me pass quietly and unnoticed, as I had lived, onto somewhere better. But the sun had other ideas, and it rose (stubborn as ever) and found me lying on a cold bathroom floor, unable to get up. Quite convinced that to do so would be nothing more than a waste of everyone's time, most of all mine.

It's been three months since my big sister suggested I should spend some time with Troy. She said no matter what I had been through, I was still an uncle. And that was a thing that meant something. I haven't been a good uncle to the kid over the years. Not that he's accrued many, he's only five. But I would've liked to have seen him more.

One of the things about trying unsuccessfully to have a child of your own, for a long time, is that eventually you stop wanting to be around other people's. It's just too difficult. You develop a tendency to frame their every action as a significant moment in a parallel version of your own life, the one which you are not living.

Troy is a great kid, but for a while now my sister has been concerned about his "development". I'm not really sure what they're expecting him to develop into and I don't think they know either but for some reason they're worried that the process is happening too slowly. My sister and her husband intend to have Troy tested in some way but they've not been very clear on what that may entail.

I've always liked Troy, I like the way he looks at the world. He interprets things in his own unique way, which unfortunately is usually a surefire way to get yourself labelled as requiring of "analysis", especially if you're a kid.

He gets words slightly back-to-front, perfectly normal for a five year old. He doesn't really understand plurals, also not a big deal.

So he'll say things like, "Can I have a crisp please?" My sister will patiently correct him, "Troy you say can I have *some* crisps, or *a packet of crisps.*" When for all she knows he might've just wanted the one.

He'll say, "Mummy my hairs need a cut." And she'll say, "You just say *hair* sweetie, not *hairs.*" Of course this makes absolutely no fucking sense whatsoever so it's no wonder the poor kid is slightly confused.

Troy likes music, and I play the guitar in a band, or at least I used to. My band, Furious Dad has never officially broken up. But we haven't played together for a long time and I think we all know those days are over. Adam went on to undertake a never-ending PHD which will probably be no use in the "real world." Steven works in a dismal sales job for reasons not even he understands. I'm a total fuckup who can't deal with grief or process adult emotions properly. Nick is happily married, and a parent.

You know how it goes I suppose, the first person in the group has a baby and it's all fun and new and exciting. The mum turns up at band practice with the kid in a little baby Ramones t-shirt and it's great—you're like three uncles to this new kid who's joined the gang. Then it starts getting a bit harder for that one guy to do stuff but you can't object, a baby is pretty important after all. Then one by one the others start to find things in their lives which are more important than the band you all helped create together—this thing that was more than just a hobby, that at one point you all honestly believed was going to be the thing you all dedicated your lives too. Soon it all changes and eventually you've got no one left to play guitar with and it's just not as much fun on your own.

I like to play guitar with Troy—he's a good audience, he gets it. Once I was sitting in my sister's kitchen, playing a guitar belonging to her husband Derek which he keeps saying he's going to learn to play (so far he never has) and Troy had some homework to do. That's right—actual fucking homework! The kid's only five and labelled "developmentally challenged" and he's got to do homework. It's just some simple sums 2+2=4 and my sister says, "Hey sweetie why don't you ask your uncle?" and Troy says, "Uncle, will you sing it so it means me something?" Now my sister thought, and you might agree, that Troy had mixed up his words there but I don't. I think he meant what he meant and so I made up a little melody on the guitar and sung the sums to him a few times (I'm not much of a singer but he doesn't know) until he started to join in. We made a little refrain out of,

"2 plus 1 is 3
3 minus 1 is 2
2 plus 2 is 4 and takeaway 2 and that's still 2"

God knows if he remembered it but hopefully it meant him something.

One day he'll probably start singing in class and get sent straight to the headshrinker, the poor kid.

Troy has never been a big fan of clothes. For some reason he tries to take them off at every available opportunity and can get quite agitated when my sister tries to make him wear trousers. This is not without its inconveniences (for my sister I mean, not for Troy) once you've had to capture a five year old kid running round a cafe in just his pants, you tend to stick to eating at home.

I know how he feels—sometimes you just want to be free. He seems to prefer the cold, and I kind of get that, in a way. Just the right amount of cold is peaceful. Maybe that's what he likes.

So I made sure that the first time I took Troy out for some uncle/nephew time (if that's even a thing) that it was a cold day. I took him to the zoo to see the penguins. It was a freezing cold day in November—bright and sunny. The sky was an endless blue horizon and the frost twinkled like memories.

I like penguins. They were one of the last things I thought about, while I was lying on my bathroom floor, freezing and unable to move. For some reason I thought about penguins then, as the alcohol and barbiturates really began to take hold. I thought of how those plucky, flightless birds huddle together for warmth while the icy winds batter them. I thought of how I no longer had another penguin to keep me warm.

"Where are the penguin Uncle?" Troy had asked as we looked at the still blue pool in the middle of the frosty zoo enclosure with its two intertwining slides traversing above the water. *What is the plural of penguin?* I thought to myself. *Is it just the same, as in sheep?* Could be.

"I don't know bud. Think they might be having their lunch."

Just as we were about to abandon the penguins, all of a sudden, music started to play. Chugging power chords over a 4/4 backbeat. It was hard to tell exactly where it was coming from. Then Joey Ramone started to sing *"Twenty, twenty, twenty four hours to go-oh-oh ... I wanna be sedated."* Troy's little round face stared up at me, his eyes wide beneath his bowl haircut as he searched mine for an answer to what was going on. I just stared back 'cos I didn't know.

As the Ramones blared out of unseen speakers, one by one the penguins started to emerge. They came from either side of the pool, out of small hatches built into the walls. They shuffled along close to one another almost perfectly in time to Tommy Ramone's drumbeat. There were all different kinds of penguin. Some big, some small, some with little tufts of feathers on their heads that looked like ears. After they marched out they all started to jump in the water and swim across the pool. Once they popped up on the other side their keeper would throw them a fish from a bucket. They came careening down the slide, splashing and sluicing in the water as Troy and I watched on, the sun shining down on us, our breath pluming like ghosts in the air.

"Just put me in a wheelchair, get me on a plane
Hurry hurry hurry, before I go insane ..."

It was my sister who'd pulled me off the bathroom floor. Got me to the hospital. Sat with me once I woke up and held a straw to my chapped lips, to help the icy water go down my torched throat. And gradually, the cold began to leave my bones. And it helps to remember that no one can withstand the cold on their own, but together you've got a chance. If you huddle together like our penguin friends you can keep each other warm enough to survive.

Today me and Troy are in a flower shop, looking for some flowers for my sister. We've been to this one a few times—Troy likes the flower shop because it's cold. I like it when he asks me the names of all the flowers and I just make them up.

"What's this one?"

"Buggle Hop."

"What's this one?"

"Twisty McBendyson."

"What's this one?"

"Pink Ears."

"What's this one?"

"Keith."

This will go on for some time. The woman behind the counter smiles. I like making up the names, I don't think it really matters to Troy what I say.

Just as long as it means him something.

COOPING MECHANISM

how much chicken wire
must you wrap around yourself
before you realise
it ain't the fox
that's the problem

POP MUSIC IS THE IDEAL MUSIC TO RUN TO

I push the speed of the treadmill up to 14km/h and increase its incline to level 3. I aim to run 5km in around 23 minutes, to finish my workout. I've chosen a treadmill directly in front of the big wall of mirrors so I can watch myself run. I'm in all black Nike gym gear and trainers. A silver St. Christopher hangs around my neck and bounces off my rock-hard chest. There's a slight sheen of sweat on my skin, which combined with my tan, makes my muscles look even more defined.

By anyone's standards, I look pretty incredible.

Pop music is the best music to run to. It's all because of the number of beats per minute, which for most upbeat pop tracks is between 130 and 150 beats per minute—apparently the human brain responds positively to this kind of tempo. It has a tribal, shamanic effect on us—invading our central nervous system and compelling our bodies to move in rhythm with the music. Perfect for dancing, fucking and running.

It also helps to drown out unnecessary thoughts from your brain. Why do you think an army marches to the beat of a drum? It's not just to keep you in step, it's to keep your brain focused on one thing—moving forward. Transforming your body is a slow process, the gradual carving away of your old self, to create something new. It's painful, and if you stop for too long you'll realise that actually, none of what you're doing matters. So just listen to the beat, and don't stop.

I've got a slight pain in my left ankle today, just a twinge. A good thing, because it reminds me of the sacrifice required in order to change. I invite the pain in and make a point of slamming my left foot down onto the treadmill as hard as I can, in time with the music so it courses right through me like electricity, amplified by the bass and kick-drum.

The gym is quite busy for a Wednesday morning. The usual crowd—botoxed yoga mums, city-boys jacked on steroids sweating out last night's cocaine, varicosed-veined old people trying desperately, pointlessly to evade death and of course, beautiful women.

I like to watch women at the gym, and I think they like to be watched.

Women love to be pursued. For this reason it's hard not to think of them as prey. But prey that wanders willingly in front of the hunter doesn't think it has anything to fear. Sure, they know we can overcome them physically, but that's out there—in the dark alleyways and dingy nightclub bathrooms. In the newspapers and the apocryphal tales. It doesn't really happen, not to these women, they're safe and they know it.

If anything, it's us who should fear them—spiteful creatures, capable of inflicting pain far more severe than anything wrought by something so trivial, so meagre, as physical injury. People laughed at Douglas. That's because Douglas was weak. Weak people think they can hide. But the bullies—the violent and sadistic, will seek you out. And once you've exposed your soft underbelly then you're nothing but a feeding trough for animals. So you have to keep running, keep getting fitter, harder.

Pop music helps, it really does. So relentlessly upbeat and stupefying. Hunger is good, you should never allow yourself to be fully satiated. Loneliness is your friend. No one wanted to sit next to me at school. Now no one wants to run on the treadmill next to mine—it's a good thing, means they're intimidated.

I focus on the girl in front of me. She's been looking over in my direction the whole time I've been in here. She started doing squats just as I was doing my bicep curls and now she's chosen to run on the treadmill in front of me so she can show off the small dimples in her lower back. She knows exactly what she's doing.

I think about what it would be like to be alone with her. I try to imagine the sound of her shallow breathing. Then I picture myself weeping with my head in her lap, arms tucked around my legs as my whole body shakes and convulses.

I hear her laughing and I feel the sharp pain in my ankle which is getting worse. I smell the fetid stench of the school changing rooms after PE lessons—deodorant mixed with fear. I feel the thudding bass line and I listen to the disembodied, mechanised female voice singing the empty, empty words.

I think of Douglas, alone where I left him. And how every day I have to leave him further and further behind or eventually he'll catch up to me.

The girl on the treadmill finishes her run so I cut mine short, taking a chance she'll be heading to the pool, I want to follow her.

As I enter the sweat-scented changing rooms, the stale odour hangs in the air like a physical presence; thick and viscous in my nose and lungs.

I fight back the urge to choke, try to focus on my surroundings. An Asian guy, about my age, in phenomenal shape, standing in front of the mirror in a towel—admiring his own physique. Why not? He's worked hard for it. His abdominals are incredibly well-defined. Must be sub-five percent body fat. His waist is slightly more slender than mine, his chest and shoulders slightly broader, creating the 'V' shape of his torso (a swimmer, maybe?) his hair is shiny and black. People think Asian men are unhygienic and stink of curry, but that's not true—most of them are actually very clean and well-groomed.

There's this older guy who visits the gym quite regularly—fat and bald, apart from these mad tufts of hair sprouting from the side of his head. He's very hairy everywhere else and completely bollock-naked apart from a towel which he's inexplicably draped around his neck, as if to further emphasise his nakedness. His penis is absolutely tiny, peeking from beneath a thick mass of pubic hair. It's about an inch long, pointy and quite black in colour. It looks as though he once pissed on an electric fence and the thing got frazzled.

He's standing with one leg up on a bench talking to someone, some bewildered stranger, telling him at great length about his mobile phone contract, explaining the details—*I get ten free picture messages per month,* he tells this random guy who is desperately trying to find a way to end the conversation.

Frazzled Penis clearly just wants someone to talk to, might be the only reason he's here. As he yammers away, the image of Douglas tries to coalesce through the steam and the vapour. The way he used to speak—gulping and gasping for air as he stuttered. The kindest thing to do was just ignore him, pretend he didn't exist. I almost feel bad for this weirdo in the changing rooms but then I think fuck him, I hope he gets eaten.

I head to the pool and swim a few lengths. If I've played this correctly the treadmill girl will appear shortly. Sure enough she walks out the changing rooms in her swimming costume, not a bikini as I would've hoped for but in fact (even better in my opinion) quite a high cut, backless, white swimming costume which really shows off her muscular legs and thighs.

She swims a couple of lengths of elegant breaststroke, not looking at me at all, which I know is deliberate because she will have noticed me. It's all part of the game, she wants me to pursue her. She finishes a length and climbs the steps from the pool, rolling her hips slowly and rhythmically as she walks toward the sauna.

And that's my cue to follow.

I hang back in the pool for a few seconds, reaching down into my shorts to surreptitiously fondle myself to half-mast before I get out. A cold shower by the side of the pool tightens my skin, making my torso shine like marble.

I walk, tall and proud, into the sauna and there she is—cross-legged on the top shelf, rare and perfect like a young fawn in a summer meadow.

We sit together in polite silence, as the heat of the sauna rises gently I notice tiny beads of sweat appearing on my skin. A flush rises to my face, but it's the flush of excitement, rather than fear or embarrassment. The body makes little distinction between the two though, and in order to remain calm I have to tell myself it's ok—she is seeing the image I've crafted over many, many hours. She doesn't see the impurities and the grotesque imperfections of which I've worked so hard to rid myself: fat, wrinkles, crow's feet, plaque, milia, fordyce spots, skin tags, I could go on. But I don't think about any of it. I remind myself that what she's seeing is the superhero flesh-suit I've created for myself. She's seeing Richard, the way I was always meant to be.

I turn to her and ask, "Do you work here?" in my new voice. I've worked hard at my new voice, sometimes it's still strange to hear it.

"Yes." she replies. "I'm a PT."

"I thought so. I'm actually looking for a new trainer at the moment. I'm Richard by the way."

I extend my hand out to her and there's a split second of doubt where I think she's about to recoil and leave me grasping uselessly at the empty void between us. But then she shakes my hand, and my entire being settles back into a glacial state of composure.

"Olivia."

Of course I already know who she is and what she does. I've known for some time.

"Nice to meet you Olivia."

"What sort of thing are you looking for from a PT session?"

The use of the word *session* arouses me, I think she knows. I can see the sheen of moisture on her skin. I imagine how slippery she would feel.

"Mainly conditioning and posture," I say, using the language with which she is familiar, letting her know we're the same. "I lift heavy and do cardio but it's just the fine tuning you know? Could do with some expertise."

This is going swimmingly, I think to myself.

"Well you look like you're doing pretty well on your own, Richard."

She smiles as she says this, but it's not how they usually smile, it's too knowing. Like she sees through me.

"Well I'm sure you could show me a few m-m-m-m-moves." FUCK! I didn't mean it but now it's too late. My old voice. It's out there now like some vile odour filling the hot, sweaty sauna and turning the air inside it rancid. Everything tastes like shit.

"Ok," she says, and I can see the change in her happen exactly as she says it. She's going to laugh at me. She's getting up now, heading for the door. I think of standing up, blocking the space between us. But I can't move out of my seat, I can't even look up from the floor. Her pace quickens and then she's gone. I did it wrong, I know I did. I need to start again. I want to go after her and tell her I can do it better. I want to hold her tightly and tell her that I'm better than this, better than her. She'd be so slippery, so squirmy but I'd hold on tight. I can do better.

But I don't go. I can't. I just focus on the good things. *You look like you're doing pretty well on your own Richard.* She liked my suit. I dig my fingernails into my palms, I want to make them bleed. Richard was who she saw, until I ruined it with my stupid, fucking v-v-voice. I'm a superhero in my suit. That's what I tell myself over and over and over again.

You're a superhero in your suit Richard. You're a superhero Douglas. You're a superhero.

You look like you're doing pretty well on your own Richard. I'll hold on to that until I come back later to hit the treadmill again. *You look like you're doing pretty well* I'm going to run faster and harder than I ever have until my stupid ankle shatters with the pain. I'll run myself into the fucking ground.

I'm a superhero, I tell myself over and over and over again. A superhero. I need to run, I need the pain. I need my headphones.

Pop music will help. It really is the best music to run to.

CAFETERIA

Sticks and stones will break our bones. A paperclip uncurled becomes a tiny little knife.

Douglas drags the point across his skin—back and forth beneath the worn out woollen sleeve of his school jumper. It's a secret he keeps hidden in plain sight. In the melee of the school cafeteria at lunch time, hungry mouths of lickspittle children lick salty chip-fingers, gargle liquid sugar and belch like milk-drunk babies in each other's faces.

Back and forth, back and forth, dig dig dig. Raking a bright-red trench; bloodied carrion towed through fresh snow. A diamond stylus stuck in a bad groove; silent echo where a voice should be. He welcomes the pain because it blocks out the hunger, the bad thoughts. His mum's sobbing face when the power went out. The stiffness of his uniform, not washed in weeks. The bareness of the kitchen cupboards.

I keep a close eye on Douglas, trying not to think of these things, concentrating instead on disappearing into the blank space between the formica tabletop and the linoleum floor.

He hopes no one has noticed him stealing what the others leave behind on their plates, but of course I have. There's always one or two in every year, the ones who just don't fit. They'll become the butt of every joke, the subject of every apocryphal tale. And in this year, Douglas Fitzpatrick is the one. I watch his rodenty eyes dart around my cafeteria looking for scraps.

Dougie's got a brother, Richard, in the year above. He figured out quickly he could just take what he needed from others—money, food, pride. He has to hide behind bigger boys to do it, and he has to act as though he feels nothing; doesn't care about anything, including Douglas. He knows that within my walls a boy with his 'qualities' can draw strength from the weakness of others.

Different to his brother, Douglas doesn't know how to wield power over others, doesn't understand how to use their revulsion to his advantage. This place is ruled by fear—the lifeblood of my eco-system. I feed it on pulverised mulch and watch it spread like knotweed.

There's another small, awkward boy in the cafeteria, the only boy apart from Douglas who is sitting alone, his name is Abdul Battacharya. Something of an anomaly. I didn't have to do anything to make Abdul's life miserable, this was always bound to happen on its own so there's really no sport in it. He's different of course, some of the boys in his year have named him 'Bad Dull Battery-Charger' and what fun they have when they call him their little names.

The problem for Abdul (the real problem), is not his name or his face, it's that he's clever and he doesn't try to hide it. If he knows the answer in class he will put his hand up straight away. If he gets full marks on a test he will smile and say thank you to the teacher. Such behaviour has no place within my walls, where only uniform mediocrity is allowed to thrive. It even irritates the teachers, makes them feel ok about turning a blind eye to his constant punishment as they can allow themselves to believe he really does bring it all on himself.

Abdul has only spent a couple of years within my walls but so far, he has not been broken. To my chagrin and to my shame he's remained unwaveringly positive, nauseatingly cheerful, unfailingly kind. None of this matters because of course, soon enough—such is the natural order of things—Abdul is going to have to pay.

Abdul gets up and approaches Douglas who pretends not to notice, just keeps fiddling with his little paperclip, twisting and untwisting it and then dragging the point across his skin. The sting of his little needle is a small torment, but a single drop of ink in a glass of water will bloom until it turns the whole thing black. If hunger is pure emptiness, perhaps Douglas has found its opposite. Pain is filling.

Abdul sits down opposite him but Douglas doesn't look up.

"Would you care to have a sandwich?" Abdul says in a small, pathetic voice.

"No." Douglas replies, without looking up, still raking at his skin with the metal point, turning it nice and red. *Good boy* I say to myself. *Good boy Douglas.*

"Oh, my mum always makes me too many and she scolds if I throw them away, so really you'd be doing me a favour." I told you Abdul was too clever.

"W-w-what a-a-are they?" Douglas asks in spite of himself, in spite of what he's been taught. I love Dougie's stammer, it really helps keep the focus on him and I take every opportunity to clutch the air in his throat.

"Chicken, on brown bread," says Abdul, all pleased with himself. "I don't really fancy them."

Douglas is interested now. He's looking at the sandwich like a dog chained up to starve outside in the cold. Now he's being rescued but he doesn't know if he's being a bad boy by accepting the proffered help. *Don't do it Dougie, I must keep you pure, keep you hungry. Cruelty is your food, haven't I provided all you need?*

And then suddenly out of nowhere there's a welcome sound, "What's going on here Battery-Charger?" It's a group of older boys, lead by Darren Driscoll, a dimwitted sadist the size and shape of a door; hooked nose beneath porcine eyes and a truculent forehead. And with him is a group of his henchman including *to my deep and eternal pleasure* Douglas's brother, Richard.

Without breaking his stride and in one devastating movement, Darren slaps the sandwich clean out of Abdul's hand. "Why you trying to bum Dougie F-P, Battery-Charger?" Darren enquires politely.

Abdul doesn't speak, Douglas doesn't speak.

"I asked you a question." Darren says, letting Abdul know he is not going to be let off the hook.

"I wasn't." Abdul squeaks, he looks at Douglas for some kind of reassurance, as if he's expecting Dougie to back him up. I can see Abdul's brain beginning to process what's happening. He's a drowning man in a rolling ocean, nothing but the horizon on every side, no hope of rescue. This is the lesson Abdul needs to learn.

Darren turns and addresses Douglas directly, "Was he trying to bum you Dougie F-P?"

I can see Douglas's little squirrely eyes start to well up. And then I see the anger, the pure rage inside of him that he tries so very hard to keep down. He knows he must turn on Abdul or he himself will be punished.

"Yeah he was t-t-t-trying to b-b-bum me." Douglas stammers, his little face going red with effort. "Kept t-trying to g-g-give me a s-sandwich and I told him I DON'T WANT NONE OF YOUR PAKKI SANDWICHES!" He spits the last part out triumphantly; he's a weight-lifter who's just exerted maximum effort to beat his personal best. *Oh Douglas how you've pleased me. You kept yourself pure for me, kept yourself hungry. Let the rage out Douglas, feel the hatred, oh how you've earned it!*

"Right then. You're coming with us Battery-Charger." says Darren, hoiking Abdul up by his arms and dragging him off in the direction of the boys changing rooms. The bigger boys follow behind and Richard drags Douglas along with them by the scruff of his shirt. He needs to witness what is about to happen.

The boys' changing rooms are dank and fetid. The stale stench of sweat and cheap deodorant hangs in the air—a visible fog. It reeks of squalor, tastes of fear.

"Get him up there," Darren shouts, really enjoying himself now. The bigger boys, including Richard, lift Abdul up onto the bench that runs along the wall and attach him to a clothes hook by the back of his shirt. His stands there on tiptoes, a prisoner on display. He could free himself, but he knows it would only make things worse.

"Right then you little Pakki bastard," shouts Darren, like some demented drill sergeant beasting a stupefied new recruit. "We've got you in here because we don't like Pakkis—BUT—if you can answer some questions then we'll let you stay in our country. What's it called Rich?"

"A citizenship test."

Oh Richard, you are a clever too. You've devised this whole thing haven't you? It's a way of keeping close to Darren. This way you never have to worry do you? So much better to be part of the mob than its victim. How well you've learned.

"Right, a citniz ... a citiznen ... a fucking test alright! For every question you get right, you get a point, you need ten points to stay. For every one you get wrong, you get a punch in the balls. Ready?"

The boys all laugh mirthlessly, all except Dougie who I know is just glad this isn't happening to him.

"Question one," says Darren, "what curry did your mum cook after I shagged her last night?"

I watch as the last ounce of hope disappears from Abdul's eyes, replaced by the first needling sting of tears.

"Going to have to rush you for an answer Pakki!" screams Darren, loud enough to reach the ears of Mr Monroe, the history teacher, out walking the corridors. Monroe doesn't pay too much mind. He's busy thinking about how he's going to tell his wife he lost all their money on a bad property investment, about the bottle of scotch in his desk drawer.

"Last chance Pakki ..."

At the last second, Abdul's imploring eyes meet Douglas's. Douglas looks back at Abdul, not with pity, nor with hatred or malevolence, but with longing. Douglas is looking at Abdul the way I caught him looking at Abdul's chicken sandwich in the cafeteria.

He doesn't speak though, just holds his breath and waits for the horror to unfurl itself the way it has done so many times since he first walked through my gates.

Abdul drops his head, starts to weep silently, probably on the verge of going into shock, with shame in his little voice he manages to say, "I don't know."

"Wrong answer Pakki!" Darren cries, drawing back his fist. Douglas closes his eyes and braces himself for the terrible sound of the blow. But ... it doesn't come. Instead all he hears is Darren's maniacal, shrieking laughter, perhaps an even more horrible sound.

Douglas looks up, and sees Abdul's sheer terror has saved him from any further injury. He's wet himself. A dark patch has formed on the front of his grey trousers and the urine is starting to trickle down his legs onto the wooden bench. He whimpers like a broken animal.

"Oh my God boys look what the little fucker's gone and done! I wasn't actually going to do it, oh my days!" Darren is beside himself at this unexpected twist. This happy accident which has compounded his victim's suffering so beautifully. "Get him down boys he needs to clean off."

The boys do as they're told and unhook Abdul.

"Get him in the showers."

Darren's lieutenants throw Abdul into the communal showers where he instinctively curls up in a corner. The boys turn on all the showers and start to make their way out of the changing rooms, leaving Abdul behind, soaking wet and shivering. There's a moment where Abdul splits in two. One half is the Abdul lying on the piss-soaked floor, cowering in his shame. The other is the future Abdul, inextricably tied forever to the ghost of this moment. Whatever he goes on to achieve in life (and he'll achieve a great deal) the little ghost will always be there to remind him to watch his back, because the bigger boys will always be waiting for him.

The boys make a run for it as they spot Mr Monroe on his way to the changing rooms. The last person to leave is Dougie, who stops at the door, listening to the sound of Abdul's sobbing really beginning in earnest.

Don't go back to help him Dougie. You leave him where he belongs.

"Fitzpatrick!" shouts Monroe, who's spotted him lurking outside the changing rooms. There's always trouble when Dougie F-P's around, he gives Monroe the creeps. "What are you doing boy? I heard shouting." *It's too late now Monroe as well you know you naughty little teacher. Stop interfering in my lessons.*

"N-n-n-nothing." Douglas spits and stammers. Mr Monroe looks at Douglas with his lank, greasy hair and his hollowed out piggy-eyes. He is everything he detests about this school. This breeding ground for tomorrow's no-hopers. This petri dish of apathy.

"Really? Well we'll see about that, shall we?" says Monroe. "Wait here, boy."

Monroe goes into the changing rooms and finds Abdul still convulsing with violent sobs under the running water of the showers. He shakes his head in frustration, realising he is going to have to clean the boy up and make a show of investigating the incident. He'll blame it on Fitzpatrick of course, no problem there. The boy can barely even speak up in his own defence. He'll get detention and that will be the end of it. Battycharya's been courting trouble for a while now, this was always bound to happen.

Monroe leaves Abdul where he is and tells Douglas, "Go to the Headmaster's office now boy. Wait for me there."

Douglas doesn't go straight to the Headmaster's office as he's told. Dinner break isn't quite over yet, so he heads back to the cafeteria. When the bell rings, he will help Mrs Mackenzie by tidying the plates the kids leave behind. He'll sneak a few cold chips and a chicken nugget. Mrs Mackenzie will pretend not to notice and offer him a sandwich and Douglas will say *no thank you I'm fine.*

The dinner lady will say a silent prayer for the wire-limbed boy walking lonely down the hall. There's always one or two in every year—the unfortunate ones who come through these gates only to suffer. She prays their time will pass quickly; and in some version of a future they may find a sacramental crumb to nourish them. These poor, brave little scientists, who have already had to learn too much.

THE ONLY WAY TO MANSPLAIN IT

Three weeks since her ex-husband's suicide attempt and somehow Helen was still taking care of him. He'd installed himself in her newly renovated attic, like a manically depressed possum.

Fitting really he should now reside in the place so many relics had once been stowed. Poor David—squirrelled away where the unused, unwanted and unloved things go.

Helen scolded herself, that was a bit mean. Although frankly, the little shit deserved it. Here she was, an independent woman with a life to lead—friends, the children, the over-fifties tennis league to climb and (thankfully) sex to be had—waiting on her ex-husband like a skivvy. Bringing him tea and fucking toast every five minutes just like when they were married and David quit his job to write his novel which remained unfinished. How very like David to *attempt* suicide. The man had yet to complete a task in his life.

He'd been quiet, bordering on contrite to begin with. Now he'd regained his ridiculous male bravado, attempting to downplay it all with sarcasm and drollery. He was on a lengthy diatribe now, ranting about the futility of existence, she couldn't listen to him any longer.

"David, must you drone on quite so incessantly?"

"Was I droning?"

"Yes."

"Terribly sorry. How can I explain it? Ah! I know. Have you ever taken viagra?"

"No, David I have never taken viagra although I'm certain a man of your age has."

"It remedies two pitfalls one might experience when engaging in coitus."

"Coitus? Are you a Victorian physician?"

"It means the physical act of love."

"I know what it is David. God get on with it if you must."

"Exactly what you used to say to me before coitus. Anyway, pitfall number one is the gentlemen has too much to drink and is unable to ... rise to the occasion, as it were."

"Sounds familiar."

"Second, the man becomes somewhat overenthusiastic and the whole thing is over too quickly."

"Again, sounds very much like you."

"Well you should take it as a compliment."

"I do actually. Look, is there a point to any of this?"

"Exactly what I keep asking myself but if you'll let me finish woman, the point is, a little blue pill will help a gentleman rise to the occasion again for a second go BUT and here's the rub, if one rises to the occasion again too quickly, one doesn't fully regain the sensation. The male member is now essentially a reanimated corpse. An abomination against nature."

"Good way to describe your "male member"."

"You find yourself going through the motions, having spent all your initial passion and romantic fervour. The whole thing drags on forever and you end up a bit sore when all you really want is to go to sleep."

"SO?!"

"So that's life! After about your mid-to-late thirties. Flogging a dead horse, gaining no enjoyment or satisfaction from it whatsoever."

"Jesus Christ David that is the stupidest thing I ever heard.

Who exactly are you using all this viagra with anyway? Can't be much fun on your own."

"How dare you! Never in my life have I resorted to onanism, I'm not some sort of deranged chimp."

"Did you use viagra with me?"

"I don't recall."

"I know which times."

"Impossible."

"After your father's funeral."

"Touché! You've got me there. What a day it was."

"I'm appalled, although it does explain a lot. And ... our last night in New York?"

"NO! HA! That was all me!"

"Well that proves your whole stupid theory wrong."

"How so?"

"You were forty-one on that trip and despite everything else that happened that was a wonderful night."

"Our last holiday together."

The memory tugs at David, his features change in the moment—greyer, older. Like a photograph leeched of its chroma, or "hashtag no-filter", as the kids would say. If Depression were a band, playing a concert in some dingy smoke-filled venue, then the grubby tout selling tickets down an alley would be Mr. Nostalgia. A Classics scholar, Helen knew the word's true meaning—*an ache to return home.*

It was hard not to pity David, a man whose entire life could be summed up (by himself, no less) as one long, losing battle with erectile disfunction. But pity, was not for women who needed to get things done. Helen had no time for it, she'd wasted enough already.

"David, tomorrow you're going to have a wash and get dressed. We're getting you some proper help and you'll to continue to live or I'll kill you myself, understood?"

"How about a kiss first?"

"Absolutely not. Now eat your fucking toast."

STINKY MCGUIRK

Stinky McGuirk will not be remembered as an exceptional guinea pig. Never really more than a novice climber, his problem solving skills were in the lower percentiles for the Caviidae family. Averse to water. His aroma, questionable.

He had the appearance of a perpetually shellshocked rodent—twitchy, trembling. Bug-eyes staring vacantly into the middle distance. His ginger and white hair stuck out at every angle, like some demented throw-cushion.

The last guinea pig in the pet shop, he looked as if he needed a good home. And Jessica, suffering twin indignities of living through high-school and her parents' divorce, was in need of a loyal friend.

Dad had left in the middle of the night; the 15,000 watt security-light on the driveway alerted Jessica to the figure of him, carrying his golf clubs from garage to car with the demeanour of a much better man rescuing a Golden Retriever from a house-fire. Mum had taken to drinking Cinzano in the afternoons, weeping silently while ordering home-gym equipment off the shopping channel.

Jessica's younger brother, Dylan, had got a PlayStation out the deal. Quite the entrepreneur, he'd figured out immediately he could get Mum to buy him a PlayStation, and Dad to give him the money to buy a PlayStation.

Jessica, not blessed with such guile, had got Stinky McGuirk.

"Oh Stinky McGuirk," said Jessica, cradling the warm little sack of fur to her neck, "you're my best friend. Let's watch The Last Jedi together and eat some hay."

"How about we do some sketching first?" said Jessica, in Stinky McGuirk's imaginary, high-pitched voice.

"What a great idea!" Jessica replied, turning them both towards her bedroom mirror, the better to converse.

"Draw me like one of your French Girls." said Jessica, like a ventriloquist, before laughing uproariously to herself.

Dylan heard Jessica and came to her bedroom door to give her the finger.

"Fuck off!" she shouted back, before apologising to Stinky McGuirk, who hated loud noises. "I'm sorry Stinky McGuirk, that was too loud wasn't it? It's just Dylan is such a little shit isn't he? Yes he is." She smoothed Stinky McGuirk's fur and made shushing noises to calm him. Stinky McGuirk purred and chirruped contentedly in her arms.

All creatures on this earth need love. Jessica truly believed it. But love is merely a human construct. The same snake oil which makes us obey the Automated Teller Machine when it tells us whether we can afford to eat. The reason we sleep soundly in our beds, believing a pile of bricks and a few planks of wood will protect us from all the malevolent evil in the world.

It's an idea we choose to agree on. A higher concept designed to ensure the continuation of our own existence, however insignificant it may be. Love is the vessel we climb aboard, so we don't drift apart and drown. But the destination, the thing we're all really striving towards is something far simpler, more primal—it is merely survival.

Nowhere was this theory more evident than among teenage girls in high school.

Jessica used to have a best friend, Louisa. Theirs was a Disney friendship—a fairytale world of hair, dresses, imaginary talking creatures, a cappella singing. Which overnight had somehow morphed into the fucking Sopranos. Deep, sedimentary layers of subtext buried under vicious posturing and murderous ambition.

The wider friendship group followed a set of arbitrary rules but had no idea who made them up. They obeyed an unelected leader in Louisa, knowing her power was built on sand. They were told what to wear, who to hate, what to think. They were a pack of wolves; a black cloud of vitriol. Constantly threatening.

This week they all drank coffee, this week they laughed at lesbians, this week they were all about "empowerment", this week it was "wellness", this week they all bought skateboards.

Guinea pigs didn't come with any of these problems. Humans were difficult, girls were impossible.

Jessica knew love was not the same as need, and need was not the same as desire. She knew she loved Stinky McGuirk, because she wanted to keep him safe. She knew Stinky McGuirk was loved, because he had everything he needed.

It was desire—selfish and human—which made her start writing Louisa's name all over her exercise book in maths class on a Wednesday afternoon. She wrote it in every shape and style she could imagine, as if by tracing the outline of the name she might capture every facet of the person.

"Oh my God she's a lesbian!" shouted Francesca Belmont, who was standing right behind her. The whole class burst into uncontrollable laughter, the teacher made a cursory *simmer down* gesture before apparently thinking *fuck it* and joining in.

Things only got worse as Dad's scheduled weekend visits became more and more lacklustre. At a total loss for what to do on a rainy Saturday, out of the house, with two adolescents, he took them to McDonald's for lunch. To Jessica's horror, Louisa and her miniature McMafia had assembled there to drink cheap coffee and shelter from the downpour. When they started looking over and whispering, Jessica assumed they were talking about her, but when Bethany Davies made an obscene gesture with two fingers and her tongue, she was certain of it.

There are no guinea pigs in the wild, they exist only in captivity. At that moment, Jessica envied the guinea pigs, and longed for the confines of her favourite bathroom-stall in which she usually ate lunch. She ached to be alone on a sawdust floor in a tiny cage, asleep in a cotton-wool nest.

"How come you're not eating anything?" asked Dad. "Is it because you're on a diet?"

Dylan smirked.

"Um, I don't know SCOTT ..." replied Jessica, trying teenage rebellion on for size, instantly finding it didn't suit her. "... should I be?"

Dylan almost choked on his Big Mac. Dad just looked slightly confused, a bit like Stinky McGuirk. By adopting a foul, belligerent attitude, Jessica had hoped she might blend in with her surroundings and not be so noticeable to predators. But it didn't work, the girls were still looking over and giggling. Jessica chewed some fries and prayed for death.

After a terse car ride home, Jessica ran upstairs to her bedroom, only to find Stinky McGuirk lying flat on his back, paws in the air, stiff and cold.

"OH MY GOD!!" she screamed. Dad had come inside for a discussion about bills or something and now raced in the direction of where (he assumed) Jessica was being murdered.

"Jessica? What's happening, are you ok!?"

"IT'S STINKY MCGUIRK!"

"What? That rat of yours? Is he still alive?"

"HE'S DEAD!!"

"Ah. Well now, hang on a minute. He might just be hibernating. We could wake him up. This happened to someone else I know."

"GUINEA PIGS DON'T HIBERNATE DAD! YOU'RE THINKING OF HAMSTERS!!"

"They're all the same." said Dad, with a wave of dismissal.

Dad wrapped Stinky McGuirk in a tea-towel and placed him on the radiator. He then delicately stroked the fine white hair on his belly, up to his chin.

The whole family gathered round, eager to see if Dad could achieve redemption for his litany of failed DIY projects by successfully resurrecting a rodent. Even Mum, in spite of herself, leaned in, Cinzano in hand.

After about five minutes, just as the situation was reaching peak ludicrousness, Stinky McGuirk wrinkled his nose. Next he wriggled his toes. Then he twisted his whole body and flipped over awkwardly, like a seal. He gasped a series of quick breaths, heaving the air into his tiny lungs as everyone realised—he was alive!

"OH MY GOD!" said Jessica, not even close to calming down. "HE'S ALIVE. THANK YOU, THANK YOU, THANK YOU!"

It wasn't clear if she was thanking Dad, or some higher power. But Dad was claiming the credit, regardless.

Jessica returned to her room, cradling Stinky McGuirk in her arms as they settled in for a Sci-fi marathon.

As she cuddled Stinky McGuirk close to her heart, Jessica thought of all the poor guinea pigs who'd been buried deep in the cold ground, when all they needed was to be warmed up.

The next day at lunchtime, she didn't eat in the toilets. She bought a tuna sandwich and a can of full-fat coke and sat in the cafeteria, alone. She took out her sketchbook and pencil and spent half an hour doing a detailed portrait of Rey Skywalker, from memory. She got called a lesbian only nineteen times.

Just as she was putting the finishing touches to the piece, Louisa walked behind her, and in the quietest whisper she could manage while still being audible said, "looks just like her," before scurrying off to join her cronies.

Stinky McGuirk died for real a couple of weeks later. The low temperature and rigor mortis were once again present. But the early signs of decomposition were a clear indicator: this time, he really had cashed his cheque.

Jessica decided to hold a remembrance service, and the whole Price family—Jessica, Dylan, Scott and Debbie, gathered to pay their respects to Stinky McGuirk. They laid him to rest beneath a willow tree in the back garden. Mum read a poem and Dad read a quote from Wittgenstein which no one really understood. Everyone had a small Cinzano.

Cartesian philosophy tells us only Man is able to contemplate his own existence ("I stink therefore I am") and it is this awareness of our own mortality which separates us from our animal brethren. Maybe Descartes' words were true, or just something we choose to believe, because in many ways we are not so different at all.

We all need love, we all hope for sanctuary. But we are not all sailing—two-by-two—towards any kind of salvation. Life and nature are simply too cruel.

We are fallen birds—migratory patterns scrambled by high frequency radio transmitters. We are skinny cats with matted fur and sulphur eyes. Our shedded claws strewn all around us—spent machine gun cartridges. We are the last polar bears, clinging to life as our habitat melts beneath our feet.

And perhaps only by looking at a small burrowing rodent, and staring into the vast unknowable universe of his eyes, we might glimpse what could rightfully be called a soul. We might hope to see a truer reflection of ourselves.

Stinky McGuirk
(Some time around the release date of Stars Wars: The Last Jedi - 2021)

THE LOST ART OF LETTER WRITING

The care home has a sound. The disembodied chatter of TV gameshow hosts, a distant timpani of plates and cutlery, the tectonic rumble of industrial washing machines. The residents themselves speak in broken syntax, haunted parentheses. Mouths yawning, forgetful.

Yulya starts her shift at seven. By the time she gets her first break at noon she is exhausted. A day in this place feels like circumnavigating the globe in a submarine.

A glance at her phone. Instagram—marriages, babies, dinners that aren't just shades of beige on chipped plates. Staying in touch used to mean something, before the concept devolved via some fucked-up process into the click of a button, a digital heart against a stage-managed photo. Now we all stare at a world far away from the one we inhabit. A world that looks awfully bright, from behind a screen.

There is one text, from her mother—*come home soon.* Yulya came here to make a better life and to help her family but her resolve weakens when, with knotted limbs and bleach-chapped hands, she reads about *unskilled workers* in the newspapers, gets invited to *fuck off back to your own country* by thugs on buses.

She walks past Maurice, playing his usual game of chess. He's playing black today (playing white too, of course).

"Knight to f6 I think Maurice, Petrov defence." He looks up, a flicker of understanding, the revenant of a mischievous grin. He doesn't move the piece.

Today, Agnes has received a letter. Her face lights up expectantly when she sees it in Yulya's hand.

"Shall I read it to you Agnes?"

"Oh, yes please. Is it from Arthur?"

It's a copy of a solicitor's letter, regarding her son's power of attorney.

"My darling Agnes," Yulya reads, "I am doing well on my travels, the weather is lovely and I am working very hard."

There's a subtlety to this—keep it vague but uplifting, too many details can be confusing.

"I will be home soon dearest, I cannot wait to see you. All my love, Arthur."

"Oh, thank you," says Agnes, a little candle, glowing.

Agnes's son was here last week, complaining as usual. Practically accused Yulya of stealing a piece of jewellery. Yulya could steal anything she wanted, not from Agnes—she never would—but from him. A simple distraction, a sleight of hand, she could lift his wallet and put it back without him noticing. That's what you learn when your family can't afford food.

She pretended her English wasn't so good and let him rant. People who are used to getting whatever they want, find it hard to look death in the face or hold its bony hand.

Yulya rests Agnes's head on her pillow, smooths her cotton hair over her baby-pink scalp. The light in her eyes is beginning to fade as she slips gently back into the static. Waiting for the last faint crackle of vinyl, the scratch of the needle, before the long silence.

CRISIS ACTOR

The café, I think is aiming for a Parisian style but comes off more like a hospital waiting room. The black and white checkerboard floor is scuffed, dirty mop residue slowly dries on its surface. I count forty-three tiles on the floor—a disgustingly odd number. Five sorry looking cakes are going stale behind the counter.

Karen and I sit at a table by the window, shrouded in condensation and black mould. It's a small table and we're uncomfortably close together. If we both leaned forward our heads would clash. It's difficult to maintain eye contact at this proximity and Karen's face looks like a big fat rabbit as she munches on her salad while talking at me.

"So I told Mark, I said—listen Mark ..." she points a lettuce leaf on the end of her fork at me as she speaks, as if I am Mark. "Get me whatever bag you want for my birthday, I don't give a fuck. If there's not a fucking engagement ring inside it then I'm not going to be happy. I mean we've been together five years. What the fuck!?"

I am expected to answer. I need to engage on these matters, that's how friendships work.

"God yeah ... what the fuck?"

"Exactly. Plus every girl in his office is like twenty-three, tits like beach balls and vagina like a stubborn pistachio shell."

"Fucking hell Karen!" I nearly choke on my halloumi.

Karen stares back at me—lifeless bovine eyes beneath her ill-advised fringe—trying to cram a leaf of Lollo Rosso the size of a dishcloth into her mouth.

Then she starts to cry. Or rather, she makes roughly the same noise that a crying person would make, while convulsing slightly at the shoulders, but there are no tears on her face.

"I mean when's it going to happen for me?" she wails.

"Soon, I'm sure. You and Mark are solid."

"Thanks babes." She immediately stops fake crying. "Anyway what's going on with you?" her tone is now positively effusive, her face like a ventriloquist's puppet.

This is the reason I am here. I am the fuck-up friend and my answer is supposed to make her feel better about herself. My misery is her oxygen, I am the lettuce she can never stop chewing.

'Well Karen last week I accidentally burnt the back of my right hand on the oven and then I had to burn my left hand as well otherwise my family and everyone I care about will die. I GUESS I'M JUST A FUCKING PSYCHO KAREN!!!'

I want to say those words. I want to scream them. But instead I just say, "I've been having a tough time at work."

Karen leans forward and rests her spongy chin on cupped hands. She bats her fake eyelashes and fixes me with a simpering bleached smile.

"Oh babes, tell me all about it."

She pushes her salad away, but I can see she's still hungry.

It was the day after the spring flood, when Jack met the sad girl in the flower shop.

The waters had just subsided, to the dismay of the town's children, who'd followed its progress as it levitated swans and moorhens up to their gates.

The first bluebells began to peek from gravel yards, behind dustbins and under benches where nobody sat. Although ghosts did sometimes visit, disappointed to be remembered by no more than a polite message on a brass plaque. HELENA LOVED THIS SPOT—YOU ARE NOT ALLOWED TO SIT HERE!!! (It's what they'd pick, if only they had the chance to go back and choose for themselves).

The flower shop was almost completely hidden by the marauding wisteria which covered its door. You wouldn't know it was there except for the wooden sign on the pavement that read, 'FLOWERS FOR SALE—SHOW SOMEONE YOU CARE.' As if it were a command rather than a suggestion.

Mrs Reznik, the florist, first noticed the sad girl in the middle of winter. Every day she would appear in the shop late in the afternoon, just in time for the gloaming. The sad girl never bought anything and never spoke to Mrs Reznik, giving the florist no cause, other than her own indefatigable intuition, to suppose the girl was, in fact, sad.

Mrs Reznik had a nose for these things; a human barometer, Mrs Reznik could sense the drop in atmospheric pressure in conjunction with the sad girl's arrival. A portent of stormy weather. She didn't make a fuss, the first time she locked up at the end of the day and noticed the sad girl was still at the back of the shop, hidden amongst the stems of thistles and the birds of paradise.

Mrs Reznik began leaving a cup of chamomile tea out for the sad girl every night, in case she got too cold. The sad girl liked the cold though. She liked to be alone in the stillness. She liked to see the moon smiling up at her from the pools of water in the black buckets. Its light slanted through the storefront shutters, turning buds of dew on rose petals into tiny underwater palaces, nebulas of stars in galaxies far, far away from this one.

And amongst the stillness, the sad girl would be still. And silent too, breathing in the scent of peony and eucalyptus; breathing in unison with the flowers as they breathed with her. As if they were one respiratory system, one set of lungs. One perfect union, based on the mutual exchange of intangible things.

Symbiosis.

And then one day young Jack strolled into the shop. And Mrs Reznik could swear all the flowers turned to look at Jack, like he had just laid claim to the very air around them, as if his need of it was greater.

Jack's eyes fixed on the sad girl as she shrank back into the shadows, for she was the most exotic, the least available and therefore, the most desirable bloom in the shop.

"Hello." said Jack, approaching the sad girl as though she were a wild pony he did not wish to startle. He extended his arm to her, and at the end of it was a rose, its crisp white petals delicate as frosted icing. "I hope you don't mind me saying," said Jack (who had never known anyone to mind what he was saying), "but it's such a nice day, and I thought you might want to go for a walk outside?"

The sad girl didn't answer. Instead she looked from Jack to Mrs Reznik, who had been watching with arms folded across her apron, pruning shears in hand.

"Go, girl." she said. "Every day you freeze at the back of this shop. Let this idiot boy take you out in the sunshine, it will do you good child." Thus, it was settled and Mrs Reznik resumed her deadheading.

Once they were outside, Jack tried to show the sad girl everything she was missing in the warm and bright world. As they walked he performed cartwheels and Arab springs to entertain her, showed her his handstand and his backflip. But all the while the sad girl looked wherever she could for shade, for a cool canopy where she would not have to stare directly at such brightness.

And Jack saw that the girl was still sad.

So Jack thought of everything he found charming about the sad girl: the pale luminescence of her skin, the way it sparkled in daylight. The curvature of her neck, delicate as fine porcelain. Her eyes, fathomless pools of deepest green. He took a rose stem and dipped it in ink and then he wrote all of these things upon the sad girl's skin, and he hoped when he led her out into daylight once more, other people might see these qualities which only Jack had noticed before.

But the sad girl still seemed sad, and Jack knew it was not enough, simply to declare his love. He had to prove it. If the two of them could be joined *physically* by love, Jack thought, it meant they would be joined inexorably within the fabric of the stars themselves.

"Let us join our bodies together," Jack said, "so you might feel my love and my joy, and in our union, my joy would become your joy, my love your love and we will nourish each other and grow together."

Symbiosis, thought the sad girl, everything is exchange. All life is mutual, to be apart from it is to be deadheaded.

But after they were joined, the sad girl seemed sadder still, and even Jack could not help thinking perhaps he had been wrong, for he did not feel fulfilled. He did not feel complete. The sad girl was still sad and perhaps sad was all she would ever be.

So Jack placed her in the attic of his house, where it was always cool and dim. He draped a fine sheet of muslin over her head—a dark veil, which would shroud her from any troubles. In the roof of the attic there was a small hole, and the sad girl was able to look up through the wooden beams and the cracked slate at the starlight and the darkness and the moon she loved so well.

Jack was contented with this solution, and returned to his most carefree enjoyment of the daytime, practising his cartwheels and his handstands.

Until one day, rain began to fall on the town. And as more and more of it fell it began to turn into a storm. Soon the town would be flooded again and this time it looked as though the waters would breach the floodgates.

So Jack ran back home as fast as he could, and ran straight upstairs to the attic. When he looked up through the hatch, the water was flooding in through the hole in the roof, filling the attic like a bathtub. And as Jack pulled himself up through the hatch, he realised he was swimming. And suddenly the surface was far away from him, and beneath him was water as well, stretching down for leagues into the blackest of depths. He could see the moon and the stars up above him through the attic roof, but they were far away and blurry, and soon Jack found himself far below a surface non-existent a minute ago, unable to tell which way was up.

It rained and rained for four whole days, and the flood waters swept through the entire town, carrying old ladies on benches as it went (who didn't even notice and just continued their conversations). The children all took to the seas in makeshift dinghies, rubber rings and plywood rafts.

And in the flower shop, Mrs Reznik locked the floodgates to wait out the storm. When it was over, the waters rolled back and left behind only mud and damage. And Mrs Reznik never told anyone where the sad girl had gone.

For she knows that the sad girl is not sad anymore. Now she swims beneath the ocean waves with the mermaids and the narwhals. Her hair is coral fire, her skin is phosphorescence. Her days are cool and dim and silent but for whale song and dolphin chatter. Light travels slowly, days and time are muted.

And Jack too, spends his days upon the ocean blue. He floats atop a rolling swell, his legs dangle underneath him and his face stares silently up at the blank sky. And on nights when the moon shines down on him he glows, a jellyfish, spinelessly cradled in his own shadow.

And though the children will talk and talk between themselves, and ask Mrs Reznik to tell them the story of how Jack and the sad girl disappeared after the great flood, the stories will all eventually cease to be.

Lost like cannonballs sunk forever, into the heedless memory of the sea.

STARING AT THE CABBAGES

We dropped acid on New Year's Eve, the boys in the band—parked up in the sticks—close to midnight. Teenage cars circled like wagons; pioneers dissolving blotting paper under nervous tongues. The first hour is spent waiting, easing into the frequency of our surroundings, resonating with one another.

Then Jonny starts laughing and he can't stop. Keeps saying, *I think I've got a clown in my mouth!* Which sets everybody else off. Suddenly everything anyone says is funny. So funny it hurts, and we all have to calm ourselves down but then someone says *I've got a clown in MY mouth* and we all start again.

By now the outside world is calling to us, so we get out the cars to go for a walk. Steven pulls a ski-suit out the back of his car and puts it on, why does he have a ski-suit in there? *To keep warm when we go on an adventure!* It's an all-in-one day-glo suit straight from the 1980's, he looks like Eddie the Eagle.

Reminds me of all those years later, when we dressed Evie up in her snowsuit at Christmas. Reindeer antlers on the hood, cheeks flushed vermillion. Tiny eyelashes catching tiny snowflakes.

We walk slowly down passageways of moonlight. Avenues of trees become celestial cloisters up above us. We walk to nowhere in wonderment.

At length, we come to a ploughed field stretching off to a black horizon. Littered in the grooves there are strange shapes, weird creatures which must've fallen from the sky. We pick them up and cradle them, but they are rotten. These poor alien life-forms that could never hope to survive on this planet. They are brown, limp and slimy. They make us feel sad.

But then we tell ourselves that's how it's meant to be. We—all of us—we came from slime. We crawled out of it and we ascended; we grew wings, gave birth to light. We spawned in distant nebulas and built the heavens for our shining children.

And one day soon we'll all be slime again.

We're standing at the apex of creation. And if there is a God, truly we are it.

Hey Buddy! the guy behind the counter shouts. *I need a name for the cup. Whaddya got a fucking clown in your mouth or something?*

Sorry. I didn't know he was waiting for me to speak.

Are you? OK?

I stand rooted to the spot, just like I stood by the crib that day.

Standing in the silence of atoms dancing, waiting to burn.

I dredge my memory back through every sainted Christmas from that one to this, everything I've missed. I don't remember waking up on New Year's Day, and I don't remember how I got here.

Just a guy who stared at the cabbages for too long.

Body, blood, bone, hair, history.

The strangest trip I've ever known.

IN THE PLACE WHERE ALL YOUR OLD BAND MATES GO

Steven Anderson had left his car on the M6. Actually that wasn't strictly true. In fact, he'd left his car just off the M6. Even more accurate was he'd left his car in a field, beside the M6, somewhere in Staffordshire. And he had *actually* left it—physically. His body had flown through the windscreen when the car struck a tree and he was lying several feet away on the wet grass. His soul now rested temporarily in the astral planes between life and death, taking a break from it all, a little time out. Maybe trying to decide whether or not it was worth going back.

The day had started fairly ordinarily: Steven woke up feeling absolutely exhausted. It was a weekday (the week having already lasted fifteen or sixteen days) and to make matters worse, today he had a meeting to attend.

He was due to visit a potential new customer, to tell them all about the products and services offered by his employer, MiComm. One of the "Lead Generation Team" had set this up, they were a half-dozen poor, unsuspecting souls fresh out of University who'd been sold the dream of bonuses, company cars and career progression and who now found themselves locked in a grey room for eight hours a day, chained to a phone. The turnover rate was high; some of them immediately thought FUCK THIS and went off travelling and never returned. Or went back to University to study for a never-ending PHD, or retrained as literally anything else they could think of. Others just accepted it, gave up, stayed and, eventually, became Steven.

Steven had progressed to the role of Regional Telephony Systems Sales Representative which meant he travelled to customer meetings and had been granted the luxury of "flexible working" which meant he could officially work from home. This of course meant he spent most of his time napping on the sofa or weeping in the shower, both of which were not exactly conducive to doing any actual work or hitting his targets.

On this particular Wednesday morning, Steven had travelled to an overwhelmingly bleak industrial estate just outside of Wolverhampton, which was home to McDonald's Tyres & Exhausts and he was struck by the notion that if he were to gaze deeply into his own soul, it would probably look very much the same as this place. The firm's office was little more than a small, grey hut. With yellowing blinds hanging over every window and a steel door which looked as though it had been built to withstand the zombie apocalypse and/or the local population. A grimy buzzer hung from the wall and Steven pushed it so he could introduce himself. An angry female voice answered —

"Is that your vehicle?" It sounded more like an accusation than a question.

"The Golf? Yes, yes it is." said Steven.

"Can't park there, you'll have to move." said the voice.

"Right, actually I'm here for a meeting with Phil McDonald, my name is Steven Anderson, I'm from MiComm."

"You'll have to move your car."

Steven took a deep breath before asking as politely as he could, "Why do I need to move my car?"

"No parking out front, it's for visitors."

"I am a visitor, I have a meeting with Phil McDonald."

"What's your name?"

"Steven Anderson, I represent MiComm."

"Wait there."

Silence fell, and it seemed as though Steven was doomed to be left outside the steel door forever. The woman at the desk was presumably wrestling with a dilemma: preventing people from parking outside the building was no doubt an integral part of her job role and the firm probably had so few visitors, she simply hadn't thought of a contingency for a situation such as this.

Steven rang the buzzer again.

"Hello?" said the voice.

"Hello, my name is Steven Anderson, I represent MiComm, I have a meeting with a Mr Phil McDonald."

The buzzer buzzed and the door opened as if an absurd and completely pointless conversation had never taken place.

Upon entering, Steven was met by the contemptuous gaze of the reception lady, who had nicotine stained teeth matching the colour of her thatched hairdo, and the complexion of an old Chesterfield sofa. He instinctively decided she was probably called Pat.

"Sign in."

Steven signed in.

"He'll be out in a minute, take a seat."

Steven took a seat on furniture which looked as though it had been salvaged from a young offenders institute and waited, for fifteen fucking minutes.

He was on the brink of getting up to leave when Phil McDonald deigned to appear out of his office—a sweaty, bald head on top of a sweaty looking suit. He'd missed one of his belt loops so his trousers were almost falling down on one side.

"Steven is it?"

"Yes, good morning Mr McDonald."

"I've not got long but come through."

Brilliant, thought Steven. Off to a flyer here.

Phil bumbled back into his office and sat behind his desk, breathing heavily from the effort he'd just exerted. Steven took a seat opposite him, which was considerably lower than Phil's, no doubt deliberately.

"So you're here about the phone lines?"

"Yes, it's one of the many telecoms solutions which MiComm have to offer."

"I told your guy on the phone I'm not really interested in changing, but go on."

"Ok, well I understand from my colleague who initially spoke to you that you have roughly two-hundred corporate telephone lines, is this correct?"

"I've got two, mate."

"Two?"

"Yep. One for me and one for Pat."

"Ok, no problem at all, we can still give you pricing for those."

"How much could you save us?"

"I'm sorry?"

"I'm not really interested unless it's going to be cheaper."

Steven had been in this situation many hundreds of times. There was absolutely no point in continuing with the sales pitch but he felt as though he had to anyway because he wanted to take up more of this guy's time than he was willing to give away. The proper thing, the dignified thing to do would've been to just get up and politely leave but Steven didn't really feel like it today, so he continued.

"Well it all depends on how you measure cost versus value. If we can take some time to understand your business model then we might be able to look at ways in which streamlining communication can actually help to drive efficiency and lead to greater profitability, as well as cutting down on wasted time and missed opportunities. Maybe we could engage some of MiComm's technical design engineers to produce a technology roadmap, identify synergies and develop a proof of concept?"

"I do tyres mate."

"Right. Would you consider an integrated Voice over IP phone system perhaps?"

"Pat handles the calls."

"I see, and are there any other remote sites or offices which we could possibly look to connect via a Wide Area Network which would provide secure interoperability between the core sites with a dedicated central internet breakout and fully managed firewalls?"

"No."

"Well ok then, two phone lines it is."

"Listen mate, just give me the price. You're all ringing me up every week saying you're the best thing since sliced bread and you can do whatever, but I've got a business to run here and I'm just trying to save some money and I'm not interested in widgets and doo-da's."

"I see well, what if I were to offer to felch you?"

"What does that mean?"

"Felching? Oh it's great, it's the latest technology. Basically the way it works is I take your trousers down, bend you over your desk and make love to you. Then once I've ejaculated inside your anus I use my mouth to suck out my own semen, and you've been felched. You look like you'd enjoy it very much."

There was a moment when Phil's face went utterly blank, as if he'd just been told the square root of purple or the weight of the universe, his brain had no way to comprehend what it had just heard. For a second Steven actually thought he'd broken him. Then, as the realisation he'd been insulted (or at least inappropriately propositioned) slowly dawned on Phil, he appeared as if he was about to have a heart attack and soil himself at the same time.

"Listen you jumped up little shit you've got five seconds to get out of my office before I knock your bloody teeth down your throat."

"So you're tempted?"

"Fuck off! Get the fuck out now. Fffgrrr ..." The last word was presumably meant to be 'fuck' but it seemed as though the ability to form words had deserted Phil in his rage. He could be having a stroke, thought Steven.

Phil was attempting to get out from behind his desk but lacked the capacity to move fast enough to actually hit Steven, who thought for a second about just standing his ground but then on reflection thought he'd probably taken it far enough. He got up and walked briskly back in to reception and turned to the sour-faced old bat behind the desk.

"Pat?" he said. "It is Pat isn't it? I can take you away from all this hideousness. Come with me and we'll sail my yacht to the

Bahamas and never look back but it has to be now Pat. It has to be now!"

Zero reaction.

"Fug errrrrrffffff!" came the cry from Phil who now emerged from his office like an angry walrus and so Steven thought it best to exit post haste.

At first he had felt a rush of adrenaline, a sudden heady euphoria at breaking the rules, freaking out the squares. But then as it subsided it gave way to fear as he started to imagine Big Phil calling his boss who would undoubtedly sack him, God knows he'd been looking for a reason for a while. Although, Steven thought, would Phil really want to relay the whole incident to a stranger over the phone? Probably not. He might be safe.

But, as he started the two hour journey home from his pointless meeting, the exhilaration he felt slowly gave way to the familiar feeling of shame. Other people his age were doing well in their careers. They had jobs they enjoyed, work they found fulfilling—trades, vocations, skills. They had friends and social events, they had money. Other people had six-packs and pectoral muscles. They worked out regularly, played tennis and ran marathons. They had wives, girlfriends and children, they had nice clean cars and went on holiday to the Maldives or Reykjavik. They had beards and shearling coats and boots of Spanish leather. They shopped in farmer's markets, free-range and organic, drank cocktails out of mason jars with friends, took group selfies, went skiing in all the latest gear, rode mountain bikes, ate canapés at business events and weddings, had sex with each other, slept well in thousand thread-count cotton sheets on pocket sprung mattresses, read books, had flatscreen TVs properly mounted on their bedroom walls, log burners in their living rooms.

Then he drove his car off the road and smashed it into a tree, while The Ramones played on the stereo.

Steven looked up into a perfectly clear, blue sky. One of those rare and beautiful days when it's both freezing cold and sunny. The fresh air filled his lungs and he could see his breath when he exhaled. He was lying on his back with his arms and legs outstretched, he wiggled his fingers and toes and was reassured they seemed to be attached and working.

Presently, Steven's senses became attuned to their new surroundings. There was a slightly salty smell in the air - fishy almost - and he could hear the sound of splashing water. He sat up and noticed he was wrapped up well in a Gortex jacket with faux fur hood. His hands encased in cosy mittens. The cold nipped at his ears but it was not an unpleasant sensation, it was nice to feel something.

He sat, and then stood up and looked around. The blue sky continued forever in every direction completely uninterrupted by anything on the horizon. In the foreground though, Steven could see a very large circular pool, set deep inside a white marble floor. Above the pool was what appeared to be a slide, which wound its way around in an aquatic helter-skelter, albeit one slightly too small for humans.

Suddenly, music began to play. It seemed to come from nowhere yet it was all around—'Beat on the Brat' by The Ramones. As the ferocious opening bars resonated from everywhere, the scene became even stranger as what appeared to be a door opened out of the blue wall of the horizon and a troupe of penguins waddled out one by one.

The penguins all made their way over to the slide and shot down it on their fronts, diving into the pool at the end and sluicing through the water before jumping back out and starting again. The penguins were all different shapes and sizes—every kind of penguin there is—and they all looked as if they were having a great time, waddling around like drunk toddlers.

Steven threw them some fish, from a bucket which had just appeared at his side.

"Here you go Charlie, Dave, Phil, all of you guys deserve fish. Kevin, here you go. Chris! My man, have some fish. Dave you've had yours, ok fine have one more."

For some reason a small black cat now appeared right next to him as well. It looked up at him inquisitively, then started wrapping itself around his legs and purring. Steven offered it a fish from the bucket but the cat didn't seem bothered.

"Eh!" came a voice from behind him, and Steven suddenly felt a harsh slap on the back of his head to accompany it. "What are you doing idiot boy?"

It was Mrs Reznik, the woman who lived in the flat above Steven's and who ran the local flower shop. Steven had said hello to her in the hallway a few times but had no idea what she was doing here.[1] Mrs Reznik had a short bob haircut and wore moon-shaped spectacles. She was dressed in a magnificent coat of white feathers.

"I don't know." said Steven, deciding to just accept this new development. "I'm just watching the penguins."

"You are always *just watching the penguins* boy."

"What do you mean?"

"Always watch the penguins and never *am* the penguins, this is your problem."

"How am I supposed to *am* the penguins?"

"Listen idiot boy. You are too busy always worrying and feeling sorry for yourself, yada yada yada I am so sad and everyone is so mean to me and everything goes wrong. Do you think this is good? Do you think anyone would want to watch a penguin if they were always so sad and moping around?"

"Well no probably not but I have real issues and ... stuff."

All of a sudden Steven just couldn't find the words. He looked at the penguins jumping and diving and swimming and sliding to the joyous backbeat of The Ramones. How could anything even be wrong in life while this was going on? Problem was, Steven didn't know if he was actually alive.

"Am I alive Mrs Reznik?"

"No."

"Am I dead?"

"No."

---

1 Like many eccentric older ladies, Mrs Reznik frequently patrols the astral planes. The younger generation of today are very accident prone and usually lack the faculties to properly deal with these situations. The best thing for them, in most cases, is a stern talking to. And that was exactly what Mrs Reznik was in the business of dispensing. Plus, she quite liked Steven, he had neat hair and didn't make noise, but he was clearly an idiot.

"Am I ..." there wasn't really a third option was there?

"You are a waste of space is what you are boy. Not really alive, only exist in the world taking up space and time and never doing anything. Why you no longer play in band? Why you no have girlfriend? Why you hate yourself so much? Why you spend so much time crying and masturbating in shower?"

"Whoah! Look, you ask a lot of questions ... I don't know. I suppose I just feel everything is completely pointless and no one really likes me."

"This is because you do not like yourself idiot boy. Look at penguins, so stupid. Only want to swim and eat a fish and listen to nineteen-seventies punk rock bands all day, this is their life. They are happy though, they love all this and so everyone loves them."

"So you're saying I should try to imitate the penguins?"

"No."

"But you just said ..."

"I am not telling you anything, idiot boy, you have to work out for yourself, I am not your Fairy Godmother."[2]

"Ok, I get it, the penguins are happy as long as they've got fish and a slide and the Ramones and maybe that's enough for them but they're penguins. I'm a human man, it's different. Maybe I just expect more out of life."

"My husband, he expected more out of life. Every day I would cook for him, soup and dumplings, sometimes with sausage, a little vodka on the side, very good. And every day he complain, *why can't you cook anything else, every day I must eat the same old soup and dumplings yada yada yada.* And I tell him, be quiet Yuri! It is soup and dumplings for you and this is what you will eat. And you know what? He just accepted it and lived a long life."

"I thought you were going to say a long and happy life."

"No."

"How long were you married?"

---

2 Incorrect. Mrs Reznik is in-fact the unofficial Fairy Godmother of all unsuccessful indie bands. She's been doing the job since the mid-noughties, when demand was at its peak. It's a tough gig, with highly irregular hours, but there's no one better than Mrs Reznik.

"Thirty-two years. Then he die in tragic farming accident, very suspicious circumstances. I collect money from insurance and move to England, so good for everyone."

"So what? You're saying, even if you don't like something, you should just put up with it anyway until you die? That's your point?"

"Listen idiot boy, when you get to my age you forget point of story as well. If you don't like it, you fix it. Otherwise carry on and fall into corn threshing machine and die, is up to you. Now give the penguin a fish and go home. Come Tabitha, we go."

The cat jumped up into Mrs Reznik's arms and the two of them disappeared along with the penguins and the slide and the Ramones and the blue sky and the sunshine.

And Steven woke up. The intense pain he felt once again alerting him to the fact he was definitely alive.

THE PRINCIPLE OF GENTLENESS

There are seven fundamental principles of Judo. The first is 'Physical Training.'

A father takes his son to Judo class on a Sunday morning. The boy doesn't really enjoy sports, much preferring to be indoors watching Thundercats on TV, he doesn't have many friends. The son will be picked on at school for being quiet, worries the father, who doesn't want to re-live his own childhood vicariously.

Kids and parents sit on benches around the mats, waiting for the class to begin. The Sensei steps out to the middle of the mats, filling up the space, the room hushed before him. The father wishes he looked more like Sensei. He thinks that Sensei looks the way a father should look; he's at ease, but ready to fight. He is motion at rest. This is 'Shizentai', the natural posture of Judo. The second principle.

"Who wants a fight?" Sensei asks the kids at the class, who respond by rushing over and jumping on him. All except one.

The boy looks at his father for a cue, some sort of instruction but receives none. *It's your choice* are the words that pass silently between them. The boy gets up and runs to the mats. Arriving last of all he stands on the periphery of the melee, just slightly out of reach of the fun. The same way he'll stand at so many parties as he gets older. 'Courtesy' is the third principle: everything in Judo must begin and end with respect. Only through courtesy can we recognise the dignity of another's personality. 'Sen' is the fourth principle, meaning *to take the initiative.*

IIIIIIIIIIIIIII

The fifth principle—'Kusushi' (breaking balance).

In Judo, victory or defeat is attained through 'Kuzushi.' It is the manner in which balance is destroyed, leaving the combatant in a vulnerable state.

Years after Judo lessons have come to an end, the father and son take a holiday together in Barcelona. The father has tried to worry less about his son as the years have passed. The boy being picked on at school, having no friends. None of these fears came true. Instead, new ones sprang up in their place.

The son is a teacher now. He still watches retro cartoons from the eighties. But they have more in common than the father ever thought they would. They both like pulling the wings off a roast chicken. They both listen to Tom Petty, read Stephen King. They're both lousy at assembling furniture. They talk comfortably of nothing in particular while crammed in at the bar at El Xampanyet, eating boquerones and croquetas, their glasses generously refilled with the sparkling wine for which the place is named.

The father feels unsteady for a moment on his feet. Just the wine, he tells himself, just the heat, it's crowded in here. Getting old, he tells himself. He's feeling much worse by the time they leave but says nothing to his son, doesn't want to spoil the trip.

The sixth principle of Judo is 'Stability.' A man falls easily if his centre of gravity is disturbed by an external force; it can be something as minor as stepping on a pebble.

After the father's first stroke, he makes a reasonable recovery, with some loss of movement. He is still able to live alone, until the first time he forgets who his son is.

"Have you come for the newspapers?" he asks him one day, his face blank and lolling and expectant, like a good-natured old Beagle, but nothing like the man his son knows.

The seventh principle, 'The Principle of Gentleness' is the overarching concept of Judo. It means that victory is not won by applying superior force but rather by utilising the force applied by an opponent. If your opponent steps towards you, you take a bigger step backwards and take him with you, using his own force to break his balance.

The son visits his father in the care home. He speaks to him as he always did, regards him with the same dignity. Tries to recognise him.

"There's a thief coming into my bedroom at night," the father says. "He wears a cap on his head." He's describing his son, the uniform he used to wear to school. It is not the first time he's said this. The son fights the urge to shout at him, "No there isn't! You're talking about me." But he doesn't. Instead he plumps his dad's pillow and props him up so he can see the TV which plays on mute all day. Then he refills the plastic cup of water by his bedside, and says he'll get the nurses to look into it.

He thinks of a passage he once read: *Death does not send you any letter, he comes sneaking just like a thief.* Perhaps the thief is real, and his father senses him getting closer to his prize. But death has already sent them a letter; he sent it to El Xampanyet on that warm night in Barcelona. Now Death is just waiting for the man to fall gently into his arms. Death is late for his own party, and where—the boy thinks—exactly, is the courtesy in that?

TOAST

We don't have a toaster in our house any more. Not since you left. Every time I walked past it I'd notice the dial was set differently, never where I'd left it. Sometimes it was set to an odd number, sometimes halfway between numbers, if you can imagine doing such a thing?

I always had to make two pieces of toast at a time—an even number—but they were never toasted quite the same. The subtleties in shade and colour would be disregarded or just missed by most (normal?) people but to me they screamed like blackened scorch marks on fresh white linen. Cried like angry facial contusions. The remainders of an equation that would not resolve itself. Variables which always added up to failure. Always too many variables.

So I had to get rid of the fucking toaster.

I put it in a box. A real life box, not one of the tiny compartments in my mind which I use to lock troublesome things away. I put the toaster in a real life cardboard box with the rest of your things when you moved out. And for a little while, it actually helped.

Molly still wants toast of course. In fact she's just asked me if she can have some 'toes' with 'peagnut burrer' as she's started calling it.

So I use the grill. There's no flame—just the hot, glowing metal bars in the top of the oven. I like watching the toast toasting, seeing the gradient change ever-so-slowly and knowing I have the power to save it before it turns black. It's satisfying. I love the bright orange colour of the metal bars when they heat up. It reminds me of the scene at the end of Terminator 2 (which you made me watch) where Arnie gives the thumbs up as he dissolves back into the liquid metal. Because sometimes I need a thumbs up. And sometimes I feel like a futuristic cyborg, sent back through time to make fucking toast and learn to replicate human emotions.

The toast is done (perfectly) but as I reach in to take it off the rack, the top of my right hand touches the red-hot bar. There's a faintly audible *hiss* as it scorches the skin and I pull my hand away, dropping the toast onto the floor.

I start to cry. Not because of the burn, it doesn't hurt that much, but because I dropped the toast onto the floor.

"Are you ok mummy?" Molly asks.

"Mummy's fine," I say, dabbing at the tears with my burnt hand, reassembling myself as quickly as I can for her sake. I don't know how many times Molly has seen me burst into tears like this. I think of you—how you would've helped me clean the floor if I'd let you. I think of the empty space where your toothbrush used to be, the cracked bathroom tile which will never be white no matter how much I scrub it.

I look back to check that Molly isn't watching me, but it's fine she's absorbed in some cartoons on TV. I take a moment to steady myself. Then slowly—with controlled breaths—I touch the back of my left hand to the bar of the grill. It makes the same hissing sound, and leaves an almost identical red mark to the one on my right. I immediately feel calmer, balanced. It's as if I've righted a car that was spinning out of control—steer into it, that's what they tell you. I lean into the pain, letting it fill me up before switching it off like a lightbulb.

I hope the burns will stick around for a while, I want to enjoy watching them heal.

When I packed the toaster away in the box with your things, I put the letters I wrote you in with it. Then I put the box in the attic.

I lay awake at night thinking the toaster might somehow switch itself on and set fire to the box, and the letters. I imagined the whole attic catching fire, flames bursting from the roof. And then all of the words in all of the letters I could never send would rise up on the smoke and turn to ash in the night sky. In front of a pale moon they would flutter down gently though the freezing air, and maybe somewhere you would taste one on your tongue, and know that I once wrote you a snowflake.

FREE TO A GOOD HOME

Before Kelly wanted to be an actress, all she wanted was to be like her mother. When she was a little girl, five or six, she'd put on Christine's patent heels and shuffle around on the linoleum kitchen floor—knee high and invisible to the crowds of grownups who occupied their home most evenings—heads wobbling and chattering above her in a cumulus of cigarette smoke.

All little girls idolise their mothers, but in the middle of those kitchen parties, Kelly felt sure there was no mother more beautiful or worthy of adoration than hers—with her blonde hair piled up and red lipstick, throwing her head back laughing at something some handsome gentleman had said to amuse her. It seemed as though the whole wide world were friends of Christine.

As the other adults noticed Kelly playing dress-up, they would join in, finding some of Christine's necklaces to put on her, making up her face with Christine's foundation and smearing lipstick across her mouth with unsteady hands.

"Oh she's adorable!" they'd sing and cackle, "I want one!"

They'd teach her to mix drinks—white wine spritzers, rum and cokes, vodka lemonades. Asked her to get up and dance with them to Madonna, Kylie and the Human League. Kelly played her part to the fullest, giving the audience what they wanted and revelling in the applause.

In the mornings, when Christine's eyes stared bloodshot and vacant at the TV talkshows and her mascara streaked its way down her face (trying to leave, same as everyone else) Kelly played a different role—a girl who had had enough sleep to go to school, who had got herself up and ready and dressed in her uniform even though it hadn't been washed or ironed, who had made herself a packed lunch from what little she could find in the cupboard, because she knew this was what her mother wanted to see.

But whatever Kelly did, no matter how hard she tried to be the perfect daughter, Christine only became more and more miserable. Soon her friends stopped coming over; she didn't dance in the kitchen anymore and she didn't throw back her head and laugh anymore and she didn't even say "well done my good little girl, you make mama so proud" when Kelly got herself ready for school in the morning because she couldn't take her eyes off the daytime TV anymore and she didn't go to the shops anymore and she couldn't even take care of their cat, Spark anymore and she gave Spark away to someone or other who came round to the house one night and Kelly loved Spark and when she came down one morning and Spark wasn't there she thought he'd run away but why would he do that? And mama explained how Spark couldn't live with them anymore and she'd given him away "to a good home" somewhere better for him to live but Kelly couldn't understand any of it because the best place for Spark to live was here, in this house, with Kelly.

Kelly who loved her mum. And Kelly who loved her cat.

And it's strange how, of all the events Kelly remembered from her childhood, Christine giving Spark away to some stranger was the only one she couldn't quite forget.

There is a pain, quite extraordinary and unique, which comes from knowing that someone or something you love is out there in the world, and not knowing if they are happy, or safe or warm and not being able to do anything other than keep them in your heart and imagine some alternate version of a future in which they have everything they need. And when you imagine, you pray. And when you pray, you promise. You promise you will gladly and willingly give up everything you have, if it means the creature you care about can have a home—can know love, and kindness.

Maybe this was what made Kelly get a job working in a vets clinic to pay the bills after she graduated drama school. During her time working on reception she got to know a lot of animals and owners and she lost count of the amount of awful cases whose narratives had begun with "free to a good home."

And years afterwards, when she was a successful actor and had worked hard to put her past behind her; to deal with everything that had happened to her. To confront her mother, to blame her mother, and finally to forgive her mother. After everything, maybe it was still the memory of Spark, that made Kelly want to adopt a child.

Tabitha was eleven years old. In her short life she'd already known more pain and suffering than most people have to endure in a lifetime, certainly more than Kelly had to cope with in a childhood which she'd always thought of as being singularly tragic in its unfairness.

No matter how bad you think things are. Things—as life has a habit of reminding us—can always be worse.

Tabitha had loved her mother; this much Kelly knew for sure. She also knew that one night Tabitha's mother had fallen asleep on the couch, and Tabitha, as she'd done on many other nights before, had lain down next to her and curled up in the crook of her arm. And in the morning, the vomit which had choked her mother to death in her sleep, was also in Tabitha's hair.

When Kelly first met the girl, she saw her looking at the world the same way a captive chimpanzee looks at the glass walls of her zoo enclosure—through eyes untaught to hope for anything better. Kelly recognised the way the girl was trying to disappear in plain sight. It was something you learned when you lived in small spaces amongst violent tempers. But her eyes did meet Kelly's, for just a moment. And when they did, something silent and unspoken and primal passed between them. If there was one thing Kelly had taken away from her time as a veterinary receptionist it was the sure and certain belief that all living creatures naturally seek comfort, or what human beings might naively call, love.

And so it was, in almost no time at all (compared with how long it had taken to get this far), Tabitha came to live with Kelly.

The first problem was getting the girl to talk. Not to "open up" or "express herself", she had a counsellor assigned who was supposed to be doing that, but literally—to speak. Tabitha had a stammer. It wasn't clear whether she'd always had it or whether it was the result of the trauma she had suffered. The only words she ever really attempted were "thank you" which was usually a complete disaster, the voiced fricative hammering relentlessly against the poor girl's teeth.

So, for the most part they learned to communicate wordlessly. Tabitha stayed in her room a lot, listening to music. She'd arrived with a Sony Discman and a whole load of CDs in a plastic wallet. Kelly bought her an iPhone and some Bose headphones and a Spotify subscription. She'd downloaded all of Tabitha's favourite artists and albums, somehow the girl had absolutely impeccable musical taste.

In the beginning, Tabitha would come downstairs only for meals, which were eaten in silence. Then she would creep back up to her room. But occasionally, as the weeks passed, Kelly would be sat under a blanket watching TV and she'd sense a presence—there Tabitha would be, waiting just outside the living room door, standing silently in the hall. Kelly would beckon her in and she'd curl up under the other end of the blanket, the two of them: bookends on the sofa, watching EastEnders or some other shit on TV.

Kelly worried about Tabitha's mental stimulation. She was due to re-start secondary school next year and it was impossible to tell how advanced she was in her studies, and Tabitha wasn't going to tell her. Then there was the social aspect—an encyclopaedic knowledge of The Cure, Joy Division and David Bowie would carry no weight with the dead-eyed denizens of Year Eight.

She bought Tabitha a PlayStation, silently cursing herself for turning to modern technology to occupy her child's brain, but clinging nonetheless to the notion she might actually enjoy it. She set it up in Tabitha's room and came back an hour later, only to find Tabitha sitting in the cardboard box in which it had arrived, arms hugging her knees, listening to Television's 'Marquee Moon' on her headphones.

Enough was enough, thought Kelly. It didn't matter to her whether the girl stayed in her room sitting in boxes listening to music all day; some people would see it as a pretty decent way to spend one's time. But if she was going to go to school then she needed to learn to express herself or they'd tear her to shreds. So even though it was going to be painful, she was taking her to see Henry.

"Good afternoon Tabitha dear!" said Henry, smiling politely from behind his thick-rimmed glasses. A decade had passed (God—had it really been so long?) since Kelly had last seen him and she had to admit he'd weathered nicely. He still had a full head of pleasantly unruly, disheveled hair which was now almost completely white. It went well with his open plaid shirt and faded old band t-shirt, a uniform of which he would never tire. Today's band was The Melvins, not one Kelly was familiar with.

Tabitha didn't respond, she just slinked behind Kelly and eyed Henry coolly, appraisingly.

"Care to have some wine?" asked Henry.

"She's eleven." replied Kelly.

"Ah, well, let's pretend I was asking you then? How are you, you silly old slag? Give me a hug for God's sake!" Kelly rushed forward and embraced Henry. It was wonderful to see him again. For a while he'd been a part of the closest thing Kelly had ever had to a family. Until it all ended, as things have a way of doing, and life swept them off down different paths which never re-converged, until now. Funny how, just occasionally it seems life might have a plan for us after all.

"Alright, enough's enough, get off. There's no point trying to turn me straight you know. Even your last raunchy play couldn't do the job!" Kelly slapped Henry on the arm and laughed in a way she hadn't allowed herself in years.

"Now, Tabitha," said Henry, "Kelly tells me you're a big music fan. Who's your favourite band."

"She likes The Cure, don't you sweetheart?"

"Ah, ah, ah ... button it Mummy dearest." said Henry, pouring two glasses of ice-cold white wine for them both. "Rule number one—if you speak for her, she'll never have to do it herself. Tabitha, you were saying?"

"Th ... th ... th ..."

"Who's the lead singer?"

"Robert Smith."

"Aha, so we're not a fan of the definite article then, ok I can work with this."

Henry had done many things in his working life, most of which revolved around helping people in some way. He was not, by his own admission, a professional speech therapist, but he did have some experience.

Tabitha had brightened somewhat after successfully naming Robert Smith, but suddenly, out of nowhere she bared her teeth and let out an audible *hiss*. Kelly was stunned but Henry seemed not to notice, as his attention was now focused on the thing which had caused her reaction.

"Ah! Here she is, here she is. Hello my little darling have you woken up from your nap? Yes, yes, yes, good girl."

Henry was talking to a brown and white Cavalier King Charles Spaniel who he now scooped up into his arms and kissed repeatedly on the forehead. The dog's tongue lolled out of its mouth, its eyes bulged in its head, its back limbs flailed around before Henry cradled them to his chest.

"Meet Miss Chablis Grand Cru!" said Henry, bursting with pride.

"Oh for God's sake Henry. Can't you ever just call them something normal?"

Kelly scratched the dog obligingly behind the ear. Tabitha

kept her distance, not keen on the dog at all—Kelly made a mental note.

"Tabitha," said Henry, "why don't you go and make yourself at home in the living room through there. Me and your mum will be through in a minute. Chablis will go with you, go on my darling."

Tabitha slinked off to the living room, closely followed by Chablis, eager to get to know their new guest. Kelly stood frozen to the spot in absolute consternation while Henry (a typical man) had no idea of the gravity of what he'd just said and simply swirled his Viognier in his glass before sticking his nose in it, savouring the rich notes of lychee and elderflower.

"Henry." said Kelly.

"What?"

"You just referred to me as "Mum". We haven't done it yet, officially. I'm not sure if I was ever going to."

"Ah, yes. Well now it's done isn't it? So you don't have to spend the rest of your life worrying about it. Now look, the poor girl does seem rather introverted and this stammer won't help. Have you thought about changing her name?"

"What? Why on earth would we do such a thing?"

"Because darling, the one word stammerers find most difficult is their own first name. And think how many times she'll have to say it when she's starting school."

"Oh bugger. I hadn't thought of that."

"Yes, it's a tricky one. I've met quite a few stammerers who've changed their name to something easier, and she does seem to have trouble with her T's. Plus, you know—a change of name can actually give people the little extra confidence they need. A new identity, gives them back a tiny bit of the power they've lost, I suppose. It's all to do with perception—ours and other people's. What's the old adage? Whether you're a confident person, or whether you've just become very good at pretending to be confident, the effect is exactly the same. You pretend to be an actress so you should know what I'm talking about."

Kelly slapped him round the back of the head this time. Funny, she thought—you meet maybe a couple of people in your life with whom time does nothing to dull the friendship. You'll always just be able to pick up straight where you left off.

"I worked with this one chap quite recently who'd taken a new name," Henry continued. "Idolised his brother from what I recall. Then his brother died in an accident, hit and run or something, and so my guy changed his name to his brother's name, just found it easier to say. He was called Richard and his brother was called Douglas, or maybe it was the other way around. Anyway, nice guy, very handsome. Gay, so don't get any ideas. Took a long time to realise it though. You'd like him."

"We're not changing her name."

"Fine, whatever you say. Let's go and see what we can do for her then."

Henry's house hadn't changed much since Kelly had last seen him. The living room was an expression of the man himself—chaotic yet comforting. The ceiling had low wooden beams, and a log-burning stove crackled in the hearth. Stained-glass Tiffany lamps balanced on stacks of dusty old books. Expensive looking throws casually strewn about the room, mainly (Kelly suspected) for the dog.

Tabitha was sat in the corner of a well-worn, bottle-green sofa, pressed right up against the arm; Chablis sat facing her—tail wagging furiously—trying desperately to make friends. Kelly took the battered armchair by the fire and Henry plonked himself down on the floor, glass still in hand, looking up at Tabitha and Chablis. He didn't speak, seemingly testing to see whether the girl was capable of initiating a conversation.

Tabitha, realising all of the attention had shifted towards her, looked around the room for a distraction. Her eyes quickly scanned and measured her surroundings (Kelly had seen her do this before, like a bodyguard or an ex-marine in some cheesy action film who instinctively checks every room for entrance and exit points) before coming to rest abruptly on an ornate, silver photo frame which sat alone on the wooden mantelpiece above the fire.

The photo contained within was grainy, black and white, slightly blurry. It was of a man sitting cross-legged on the floor, listening to music on large headphones plugged into an old Hi-Fi unit and a vinyl turntable. At his feet were the discarded sleeves of several 12" vinyl records. The man was looking down at the floor but you could just about make out his face, smiling. The audio equipment certainly predated the man, but to Tabitha, it all looked old.

"Who's he?" the girl asked softly.

"Ah," said Henry. "Our friend, Jeff. He's the reason your m ... Kelly and I, are friends."

"Where is he now?" asked Tabitha.

"Well, it's quite the story. He's actually conducting a research mission, in deepest Africa. Living amongst the Werawe Tribe of the Great Savanna."

"Henry ..."

"They live in the long grass of the Great Plains, you see, and they're naturally very short people, like Kelly here. So they're always getting lost and jumping up and down shouting "Werawe!? Werawe!? Werawe!?""

"Henry!"

"What?"

"You can't tell that joke anymore, especially not to kids. It's racist."

"Er ... don't think so. The Werawe Tribe are short. Short isn't a race."

"Well it's cultural appropriation then."

"In what sense?"

"Just stop it."

"Fine."

"He's dead isn't he?" said Tabitha.

Kelly looked at Henry, feeling as though she should apologise for the bluntness of the child's question. Ready to take full responsibility if any offence were caused. How quickly this newfound parental anxiety had consumed her.

"Yes," said Henry, with a kindness to his voice, not wishing to lie to a girl who clearly did not need to be protected from the truth. "Yes, I'm afraid he is sweetheart. He was a wonderful man."

Kelly reached over and took Henry's hand, as they both held a moment for their friend.

"H ... he ... he ..." Tabitha sounded like she had the hiccups. "He's still with you though," she managed to say.

Kelly felt the familiar stab of pain for this poor girl. She had obviously been told this herself, many times by well-intentioned people and now she was repeating it to try and comfort Henry, a man she had only just met. Amazing how children who had suffered so much, still held such a huge capacity for empathy.

"He's your eyes in the darkness."

Well that was a surprise. Tabitha didn't stutter or trip over those words. She spoke them clearly, definitively. And suddenly Kelly could swear the afternoon sunlight in Henry's living room had been turned down a little, and the orange of the fire and the reds, yellows and greens of the lamplights all seemed to glow a little brighter.

Henry felt it too, as though the whole universe had just been dimmed and a single spotlight had fallen upon this living room stage and these four players—two middle-aged friends, a young girl and a spaniel. And at once they were aware, every single thing that had been, or ever would be, were all just threads intertwining. Their lives were a tapestry, and up to this point they'd been standing too close to it, looking only at the individual strands, but now, once they stepped back, they could begin to see a picture. They were moving along the same vectors, travelling together through the astral planes.

They could see Jeff, listening to vinyl records on headphones. Jeff who hated having his photo taken and always refused and so Henry had captured this singular shot, when he was perfectly at peace, his face and mind serene. And Kelly could see herself as a little girl, winding around the legs of the guests at her mother's parties—ghosts of an aperture now, spectral in framing.

And both adults would spend years pondering what the girl had said—*your eyes in the darkness.* Did she mean eyes watching over you? Maybe, but the dead lacked agency, and their counsel was worthless. And it was sad to think of a soul forever watching, longing for what it could not have. Eventually they would each arrive at the same notion, quite separately and years apart—that the eyes in the darkness are the eyes only we can see, quite unique to all of us. Eyes shining brightly in the darkest of places, if only to let us know we are not alone.

"I tell you what ..." said Henry, clapping his hands together. "Tabitha, would you like to help me give Chablis her biscuits?"

The girl looked at Kelly, and nodded her head.

"Excellent," said Henry, "let's all have biscuits. Except, instead of biscuits, I think I might have gin."

"Make that two," said Kelly.

CRAB BUCKET

Just call me Uncle Crab Bucket, I knew this was a good idea. I've taken my five year old nephew Troy crab fishing. He's still not talking that much, and my Dad took me crab fishing when I was younger so I thought it might *bring him out of himself*, as people are fond of saying. As if *out of yourself* is somehow the place to be.

It's a beautiful day, and we arrive early—keen as clams (if that's a thing)? The sun looks like a sherbet lemon in a cellophane wrapper and it warms our necks as a chilly sea breeze stings our faces, reminding us to be thankful for good weather and good fishing. Overhead, gulls call to one another expectantly, as if providing a pre-match commentary, *"And it's the relatively unknown pairing of Troy and Uncle Crab Bucket stepping up to the plate, what kind of performance can they produce today? The crabs look up for it, old scores are there to be settled, and it's live!"*

There are gift shops dotted around the harbour selling crab fishing lines, bait bags and buckets and we choose one at random, the bell above the door heralding the arrival of the two intrepid fishermen. Troy is drawn to a selection of seashells on sale in a big wicker basket; sea urchins, conches, scallops, molluscs and mussels—4 for £5 or 8 for £10. Seems like a good deal. Troy picks them up one by one and asks;

"What's this one?"

"Scabby Urchin."
"What's this one?"
"Squid Nose."
"What's this one?"
"Kraken Sphincter."
"What's this one?"
"Phil Jones."

We do this a lot. This cataloging of items seems to have become our primary means of communication.

"What's a crab?" Troy asks.

Hmm. *It's kind of like an underwater spider with armour plating and claws if you can imagine such a thing?* Doesn't sound great. Luckily there's a cartoon picture of a friendly looking crab on a sign in the harbour that reads, "Absolutely NO CRUELTY to crabs whatsoever." I point it out, "That's a crab right there buddy. We're going to see how many we can catch in this bucket." He looks fairly indifferent to this proposal.

No Cruelty I think. Besides tricking them with bait and dragging them out of their underwater home into the terrifying alien world above.

I'm trying to give the kid some experiences he'll remember fondly. I remember crab fishing with my dad so I'm trying to pass that on to Troy. 'Making memories' they call it—as if you can somehow pre-emptively manufacture nostalgia. As if you even have any control over what you'll remember and what you won't.

Before Troy was born, his dad, my brother-in-law Derek, took my sister Sophie on a trip to Florence. He wanted to visit one of the jewellery shops on the Ponte Vecchio (that's a famous bridge to you, me and Troy) and buy a pocket watch. The idea was he'd give the watch to Troy on his wedding day. I thought it was quite a bougie and pointless thing to do, just an excuse to go on yet another holiday. What if Troy never gets married? It's not the most important thing in the world. And the watch would only really mean anything to the people who bought it, to Troy it would mean less than a bucket of crabs.

At the foot of some stone steps set in the harbour wall, we find ourselves a small pontoon which juts out into the bottle green sea.

The little boats and yachts bob up and down on the tide and it's not long before we can't tell if they're moving or we are.

We attach a bait bag full of sardines to our crab-line, unspooled from its orange bindle. We drop it in and let it sink right to the bottom because—and this is important—crabs don't swim. Then we stare at the tiny ring of water tension around the line—like snipers on a rooftop, looking down a telescopic sight, eyes trained.

After a few minutes we pull up the line and sure enough, there's three creepy crabs attached to the bag. I carefully manoeuvre them over to our bucket, filled with a little sea water for comfort, and drop them in. Troy shouts with delight when he sees them, jumps up and down excitedly in his little converse trainers.

After about half an hour we've got a bucket full of crabs. All floating around each other in an underwater forest of spindly black legs and pincers. To me it looks kind of dark and threatening, I can't help but imagine sticking my hand in. I hope Troy doesn't feel the same and I think to myself *you just never know if what you're doing from one second to the next is fucking them up in some unpredictable way.* I never signed on for this, which makes it so much harder.

We bring the bag up again and there's a big daddy attached. I mean this guy's a whopper; three times the size of the other crabs we've caught. I try to delicately guide him towards the bucket but he drops off onto the floor and starts scuttling back to the sea, trying to escape the bucket.

"No!" Troy shouts and reaches out to grab him. The big daddy stops and turns towards Troy, claws raised like a little soldier—ready to defend himself. I throw an arm across Troy to stop him going any closer, getting his finger clipped off. "No!" he shouts again and I realise I need to rescue this moment.

I reach round behind the crab and pin its body to the floor with two fingers. Then I scoop my thumb underneath and pick him up, so his claws are facing away from me and he can't nip me. I hold him up for Troy to see. The big daddy looks as though he's waving and Troy laughs hysterically. *Absolutely NO CRUELTY whatsoever* I think as I toss the big guy into the bucket.

I want Troy to remember this as a happy day. I want all his memories to be happy. I want him to live in a world where gulls sing in an azure sky while a sherbet lemon sun warms us. Where crabs bid you *good morning* as they jump politely into your bucket. Where sons grow up and get married and get pocket watches from their moms and dads and where nothing can hurt them.

I've got that pocket watch now. I keep it in a shoe box in my closet along with a few other small things that were worth holding on to after the accident. I will give it to him one day, because by some cruel alchemy of fate, it now holds *real* significance.

Maybe this day will be significant for Troy. Maybe not. But at least we're here together and that's something.

We admire the contents of our bucket. "Whaddya think bud?"

Troy smiles, just a crooked tilt of one corner of his mouth, but I've learned to recognise it as an indicator that he is happy, at least in the moment. His moon-pool eyes look up into mine and an unspoken affirmation passes between us—*good catch.*

We empty the bucket out and the crabs all start the mad dash back to the sea.

"What's that one called?"

"Bob."

"What's that one called?"

"Bob Two."

"What's that one called?"

"Robert Bobbington."

"What's that one called?"

"Bob Robertson."

The crabs all drop off the edge of our little jetty and splash back into the sea, floating back down to the cool depths, relieved to get back below the surface and forget about the world above.

It's nearly time for us to go. The tide is still coming in, the water is rising steadily and in a few minutes our little platform will have disappeared. If we stay for much longer the water will fill our boots, if we wait around for high tide we'll be completely submerged.

TRIFLE

When David left the oncologist's office that afternoon, for some reason all he could think about was his internet browsing history.

The meeting had been convivial, jovial almost. David making his usual joke about, 'Oh what happens when we get to stage five doc?' But of course he knew there was no stage five. The joke wasn't funny, it never had been. And now the time had truly come to 'set his affairs in order' a phrase he'd heard many times but never really considered the meaning of until now, which is why he couldn't stop thinking about his internet browsing history.

"All men have secrets and here is mine, so let it be known ..." Morrissey had sung before he turned into a bloated, pompous, right wing douchebag. He'd been David's hero, oh well. But David didn't want his secrets to be known. As a matter of fact he saw it as an achievement: he'd made it to the end of his life with the majority of his secrets still intact.

What happens after you die? Do all your online passwords go to your next of kin? He didn't know, nor did he savour the idea of Helen and the kids rifling through his credit card statements and finding information which might prompt them to set off on a quest to discover the real David, the David they'd never known, hidden from them all these years.

Because the real David was unpalatable. The 'apparent' David was the one he wanted everyone to know, the version he'd tried his best to maintain over the years, the socially acceptable face of David.

Most people cling to the idea there are perhaps one or two people in this world who truly know us, maybe better than we know ourselves. This is nonsense. No one knows who we really are, not even our closest family. If they did they'd be horrified. The problem is, nowadays, in the age of information, it's all out there somewhere, contained within our digital footprint. Which was what frightened David most about death.

He imagined Helen and his accountant having a debrief over his financial affairs:

"Look at that, still paying sixty-five pounds a month to Total Gym for peak membership. Probably just wanted to gawp at the yoga instructors."

"Well the man was a pervert Diane, let us not forget. May God rest his soul. And wait til you see this ..."

The silk knickers and hold-ups which David was wearing right now under his jeans had been purchased online only last week, from AgentProvocateur.com – what on earth would Helen say? He hated the idea of her thinking they were a gift for some floozy (although ironically she might've been more comfortable with this explanation). The fabric, calmingly smooth against his skin as he started the Volvo and left the hospital carpark, soothed his soul slightly as he made his way to his afternoon engagement.

It did a man good to have some secrets, David thought. After all, so much of life was just rather dull. All of the things we're conditioned to believe will make us happy—marriage, children, money, careers—in fact just end up making most people miserable. Because we all want more, we all crave what is outside of our daily routine, the mind numbing drudgery of existence. But—and here's the rub—as soon as you admit to those feelings, those universal and perfectly reasonable feelings everyone has, then suddenly you're admitting to being a bad person. You're branding yourself a cheat, a philanderer, a substance abuser, an addict. When in actual fact all you're doing is searching for something that will keep life interesting. How is this so very wrong?

David had never thought he was into 'fetishes' as most people would refer to some of his proclivities. He chose not to label the things he was doing. Tights, underwear, hosiery, spandex, lycra ... these things really did it for him. He'd found out quite late in life too – it wasn't rooted in some kind of childhood event or trauma, he just tried it one day and found he enjoyed it. Good to be able to surprise oneself as one got older.

A 'fetish', David knew, was originally a term for a human-made object believed to have supernatural powers. The definition made sense when he thought about it. After all, what is arousal, desire, titillation, if it's not the most wonderful kind of magic? It was something to keep one interested in being alive. Was there anything more powerful?

He hoped he would never have to explain any of this to anyone. He just wanted to go to his grave without everyone knowing every little thing about him. It would be an unbearable indignity: to have one's life forensically examined when one is not even there to obfuscate and deny.

There would be no final speeches, no long drawn out heart-to-hearts with Helen or the children. There would be no epiphanies where they realised he'd always done the best he could because the truth was he hadn't, not really, he could have done better. But no matter what, he would always be their dad, the only one they've got. Death wouldn't change that. Things don't just happen: childhoods, lives, marriages, deaths. They go on happening after the event, they reverberate through the lives of others, shaping those who are left behind. And so, in a sense, David would live on.

But today he had an appointment to attend.

He arrived at a red brick building in the centre of town. It used to be a cotton mill and now it mainly comprised trendy offices for companies who all specialised in 'digital' and had ping-pong tables and beanbags instead of furniture. David pressed the buzzer beside the name 'Roland & Threes' (he was buggered if he knew what it meant) and was granted entrance to the building. He decided to take the lift—one of those old industrial service elevators found in New York apartment buildings—to the third floor offices of Roland & Threes. Might as well enjoy the luxury since he no longer needed the exercise.

'Offices' didn't exactly capture the essence of what this place was. It was a vast, open space—beautiful dark hardwood floors and exposed brick walls (an interior designer's wet dream), brightly lit through tall, wrought iron windows. The early spring sunshine cast brilliant shafts of light in which dust motes danced like fireflies, congregating around the centerpiece—a boxing (or, in actual fact, wrestling) ring.

To its left was a hulking mahogany desk, resembling the bow of some great ship, behind which sat the owner of the establishment—a robust woman, probably late fifties, with a rhombus shaped head, a drinker's complexion and a thatch of bright ginger hair. You wouldn't have called her pretty, but you might've seen beauty in her eyes. The real beauty, acquired through a life lived to the fullest. The sparkle of it all, fired into marbles behind half-moon spectacles.

"David you old goat, how the devil are you?"

"Oh you know me Frances, good in parts."

The two old friends kissed and embraced, before Frances seated herself back behind the desk, and David on an old Chesterfield next to the wall.

"I haven't seen you for a while darling, to what do I owe the pleasure?"

"Well actually, it's my birthday."

"Oh wonderful, I won't ask how old. Any special plans?"

"Well just dinner at Helen's with the kids this evening. Shepherd's pie—my favourite."

"Oh wonderful, so good you're all getting on now."

This was all so peculiarly normal, Frances knew all about Helen and the kids but not the other way around. How different David's life might've been, how different everyone's life could be if we could only learn to be honest with each other.

"And will the children eat shepherd's pie darling? They're not squeamish vegetarians like everyone else these days are they?"

"No, thankfully not."

"What's the word for them? Snowflakes! Yes! Don't know how easy they've got it if you ask me."

"Well absolutely."

"And let's hope they never have to find out eh? You here for the hour darling, the usual?"

"Yes please. Oh nearly forgot." David handed over two-hundred pounds in cash from his wallet, which Frances stashed in a safety deposit box.

"Wonderful, you'll need to sign a waiver."

"Again?"

"Oh yes, can't be too careful darling, health and safety." Frances produced a clipboard and David dutifully signed his name—again a damn record of everything but at least it wasn't 'in the cloud' the way everything else was.

"Excellent," said Frances. "Well, all's in order, changing rooms are to your left and I'll meet you in the ring when you're ready. Safe word?"

"Vancouver."

"Vancouver, interesting. Any particular reason?"

"I just always thought it looked nice. Never got to go there though."

"Well there's still time darling. And it is nice, or at least it used to be."

"Oh? Have you travelled much around Canada?"

"Oh yes darling, went there for a while after I left the states, long before I ended up here."

"Wait a minute, are you saying you're American?"

"Yes darling. The good old US of A."

"You don't sound it."

"Well don't believe everythin' ya hear darlin'" said Frances, suddenly sounding like Daisy Duke (although without the physical resemblance) and then it was as if she were a completely different person to the one David had been paying for services (and calling his friend) for several years. What he'd always thought was true, really was: no one knows anyone. We are, all of us, merely stories we've made up and told to the world for as long as we've been able.

David undressed slowly in the changing rooms, enjoying the transformation as he peeled off his jeans and jumper to reveal silk knickers (full backed, rather than a thong) along with sheer stockings and a suspender belt. He'd opted for a camisole, rather than a corset, merely for ease of movement, and bare feet of course, the shoes were always the trickiest items to find but regardless, there was no way he was getting in the ring in heels.

David stepped through the two centre ropes and into the ring. The canvas had been topped with a thick layer of plastic sheeting and there were two buckets in opposite corners of the ring: one containing cake (Victoria sponge), and a second containing custard. In the centre of the ring was an inflatable paddling pool filled with green jelly (lime flavour, David assumed).

Frances emerged from the changing room seconds later, preceded by her enormous bosom which was crammed into a full Mexican Luchadore outfit, complete with mask and cape.

"Marvellous!" said David as she stepped into the ring. "Are you going to ring the bell?"

"Ding ding," said Frances, before flying across the ring like a rabid wolverine and throwing herself on top of him in a cross body, slamming him down into the pool of jelly.

The breath was knocked right out of David's body as he landed and Frances seized the opportunity to gain the upper hand. She slid behind David and wrapped her arms around him in a half-nelson, nearly wrenching his shoulder out of the socket.

"Ah yes, that's the stuff!" said David, through gritted teeth.

"Shut up bitch!" shouted Frances, forcing his head down into the jelly and issuing a judicious spanking to his behind. She damn near thrashed the life out of David's backside as he choked back mouthfuls of jelly, struggling for breath. There was a brief moment of respite as Frances relinquished her grip, crawling to the corner of the ring and picking up the bucket of custard which she poured all over David's prone body.

For a few seconds, David was allowed to luxuriate in the glorious feeling of the cold custard sluicing between his silken undergarments, before Frances re-entered the fray with a flying elbow to the back, forcing him deeper into the messy, swamp of desserts.

With a primal roar, Frances flipped David over onto his back, straddling him in full mount, pinning his arms to his sides with her legs. David's face was covered in slimy jelly and custard, his vision obscured as Frances leaned over and dragged the second bucket towards her. She reached in and pulled out handfuls of cake, smashing them down into David's face as he lay helpless beneath her, drowning in sugary ecstasy.

"Eat it you little hussy!" screamed Frances as she forced mouthful after mouthful of sponge and jam into David's willing mouth. David gasped and spluttered, unable to breathe beneath the crushing weight of Frances on his chest and the unrelenting deluge of cake into his oesophagus.

Laying crucified on the canvas, David began to experience the sudden rush of euphoria which he'd always heard came just before drowning. His senses began to swim, spots of colour danced in his vision before it all started to turn black. And just at the last second, too late really, he realised he was supposed to stop this; he wasn't meant to die quite yet ...

"Vancouver," he tried to say, but the word wouldn't form through the cake. "Vancouver, Vanco ... Van ..."

And then black, and then something largely black but somehow with form, and then lots of forms marching together while a 4/4 drumbeat played and power chords chugged ...

And then awake.

Coughing, spluttering, gasping for just one more breath of precious air.

"Come on darling, breathe, that's it, that's the stuff. Let's get you onto your side." said Frances, placing David in the recovery position while he hacked the cake out of his lungs. "You were down a little longer than usual this time darling I was starting to get a bit worried."

The world gradually came back into focus as David sat himself upright. He felt magnificent. For just a split second he had existed in nowhere-space. In-between the here and now and the great beyond. In the infinite astral planes which separate us from all we cannot see. He knew he'd be going back there soon, and he was more than ok with that.

"You know," said Frances, "you're not getting any younger old bean. Maybe you should get yourself a slightly more sedate hobby."

"Nonsense," said David. "I can't think of anything I'd rather do."

"Well you know," said Frances, slipping back into her American accent, "I love fishing. Fishing is about patience and perseverance." Frances seemed to have gone somewhere else, where it was David couldn't be sure. "Wrestling's all fake you know, it ain't real."

"Wrestling," said David, "is as real as real can be. Perhaps everything else is fake."

F23

Everyone had always assumed the orchid was fake. A facsimile of life, deliberately placed in an elevated position on a shelf next to the photocopier as a nod to the outside world that so obstinately continued to exist. The orchid had a way of drawing the eye, its delicate white petals visible from any vantage point, floating above the tops of the cubicle screens. Its effect was calming, in the same way that artificial images of sky are projected onto the ceilings of MRI machines, to lull the patients as they're fed into the magnetic tube.

It was only when its petals started to drop that people began to look at it properly. How could it have been real all along? It looked far too perfect. Had it always been next to the photocopier? There were some who claimed to have seen it elsewhere in the office. Maybe it had moved of its own accord?

There were even those within the office who became strangely preoccupied with the notion that until recently they had seen some other *entity* interacting with it. Some sort of moving shape which had appeared next to it at regular intervals, tending to it in the manner in which one might install toner into a photocopier, coffee into worker.

And although everyone dismissed these fanciful ideas just as they'd been trained to do, they were actually correct. The indeterminate spectral presence was, in fact, Row F Column 23 on a spreadsheet entitled 'Sustainability Assessment.'

F23 had nurtured the orchid for over two years, moving it occasionally to a new aspect within the office, trying to give it the optimum amount of natural, indirect sunlight. She'd misted it once or twice a day, placed ice cubes in its pot so as to improve absorption and ensure it was never overwatered. And once a week she'd submerged it for ten to fifteen minutes in distilled water just to give it a little freshen-up.

F23 had been Martin's PA for almost a decade. A good innings, especially as she was now past retirement age. Her two sons had been telling her to give up the job for years but she couldn't face the thought of rattling round the house all day on her own. Even though it had been years since her Terry had passed, she still didn't know what to do with time on her hands, apart from gardening of course. She was well used to going to bed alone at night but liked having a reason to get up in the morning.

"And besides," she'd say, "Martin couldn't cope without me. That man would forget to put his socks on if I didn't put it in his calendar."

Martin had agonised over the decision to let F23 go. It pretty much came down to a straight choice of losing her or his company BMW. As dedicated as F23 was, Martin had spent a lot of time and effort in choosing the Five Series. He'd specified the enhanced Bluetooth and wireless charging capability, the Harman Kardon audio system—perfect for blasting Level 42 all the way up the M6. He even had the additional lumbar support in the heated seats. His back had never felt better. The heated steering wheel had been a mistake though. It cost an extra one-fifty and actually, on chilly mornings he much preferred to wear his Dents leather driving gloves. Same ones Bond wore in Spectre. Someone had given them to him as a gift.

He felt bad about losing F23, but in a harsh economic climate, a true leader must be prepared to make sacrifices. And so it was that Martin had agreed to shoulder the burden of scheduling his own meetings, replying to his own emails and even occasionally making his own coffee so that the herd (not herd, what was the word he was looking for? hive? no that wasn't it either, never mind) might survive. At least until the next sustainability review.

He'd even gone to the trouble of arranging a whip-round for F23. He collected over £43 in total. They ended up just giving it to her in vouchers because no one really knew what she might like as a present.

After she had left, F23 was never spoken of. Most of the workers didn't even realise she'd been there in the first place. But with each orchid petal that wilted and fell from the stem, they became collectively aware of an absence. By the time they tried to water the orchid it was too late. The petals had all fallen, the roots were dry and grey.

F23 hadn't stopped to pack her things, she hadn't even collected her coat. She'd walked out of the doors and felt the sun on her face, and thought that days like this should be spent outside. So she'd gone to the garden centre and bought new gloves, some seedlings, a trellis and a trowel.

Now she sits in candied canopies of early April blossoms, while friendly bees busy themselves back and forth, and birds chatter and squawk and sing. She didn't stay F23 for long, she quickly became Orchidfan_64 and started chatting to Pruner123 who was actually called Ted. And when they finally decided to meet for coffee and cake, she introduced herself as Rose.

TO CLOAK

In spite of the situation, how much she hates the word, hates this place, she smiles a little when she sees it on the sign next to the ward.

Palliative—derived (she knows) from the Latin, 'Palliare'—*to cloak.*

It makes her think of Colin the budgie, her family pet when she was little. She remembers him singing—chirruping away, proudly puffing out his little chest. She remembers her dad saying, "Quiet Colin, time to go to sleep," and draping a sheet over his cage.

Colin would fall silent beneath his shroud, no longer seen or heard. How desperately unfair.

Strange the way that memory works—how good things can still sing in dark places. She remembers holding Colin between cupped hands; feeling his tiny fragile bones, the tick of his carriage clock heart.

In the moonlit hours, she walks the hospital corridors alone. There's an artificial smell—chemical and antiseptic, masking what is underneath. She feels its creeping presence trying to make a host of her, and she doesn't know if she will ever truly leave this place, this hinterland on the outskirts of death, this constant gloaming. Like living inside a bruise that will never heal.

The man she's loved forever, and yet no time at all, is in his bed—feverish, barely lucid. Would it be better for death to just hurry up and take him? When the time comes for her to remember him, she doesn't think she'll be able to put the right pieces back together. Him cooking in the kitchen with a glass of red wine, listening to Neil Young and Bob Dylan, singing along badly. Drinking coffee outside in the garden, reading the newspaper and complaining. She's afraid these will fade, and all she'll have left is what's in front of her now. This ward, this bed, this place.

Two days ago was the last time she heard him speak, "Pass the gin dear." It was a joke, and it made her smile. She holds on to it now as she refills his water for no reason, strokes his brow. Then she thinks of Colin, and remembers him singing.

FIN

RICK WHITE

Rick White is a writer of short stories and flash fiction whose work has been widely published in literary journals and nominated for Best Small Fictions, Best of the Net and Best British & Irish Flash Fictions. Rick lives in Cheshire with his wife, Sarah, their daughter, Luna and their Cavalier King Charles Spaniel, Harry. You can follow Rick on Twitter @ricketywhite.

ACKNOWLEDGEMENTS

Grateful acknowledgement is made to the following publications in which some of these stories (or earlier versions of them) were first published:

Anti-Heroin Chic
Barren Magazine
the Cabinet of Heed
Crack the Spine
Ellipsis Zine
Flash Frog Magazine
Lunate Fiction
Menacing Hedge
Milk Candy Review
Storgy Magazine
X-ray Lit Mag

Firstly, I would like to express my most indefatigable gratitude to Tomek Dzido, Ross Jeffery and Anthony Self, the team at Storgy Books for turning this dream of mine into a reality. You were the first to publish one of my stories, at a time when I'd received so many rejections I'd begun to question whether or not I was actually writing in English. You saw something in my work when others didn't and you've supported me ever since. Thank you.

In December 2021, Storgy launched a successful Kickstarter campaign to fund this book and three others. My heartfelt thanks go out to everyone who donated. If that includes you, and you're sitting there reading this book — you helped create something that otherwise may not have existed. That's not a small deal and I am truly grateful.

To Rob Taylor, for your wonderful cover art — it's every bit as brilliant as I knew it would be, you are such a talented artist. Thank you for agreeing to do it.

Huge thanks are also due to the editors of the literary journals who have published my work. Some are listed above but there are still more to thank — Trampset, Reflex Fiction, Lost Balloon, Maudlin House, Idle Ink, Back Patio Press, Nymphs, Sledgehammer Lit, Misery Tourism, Riggwelter Press, Honest Ulsterman. I'm in awe of how much time and effort editors and staff devote to giving a platform to new voices. Because of you I went from writing completely alone to having an audience for my work, a space to share ideas and a network of great writers to learn from.

I've met many fantastic people through the online writing community, I want to thank two individuals who have really contributed to this book. Matt Kendrick is a tremendous writer, a meticulous editor and a hell of a nice chap. Matt has provided invaluable editorial feedback on a number of my stories but most significant for this collection was his help with 'Jam', one of my favourites which I've struggled for years to get right. Thanks Matt.

Next, I simply could not have written these acknowledgments without mentioning Michael Grant Smith. Michael is one of my favourite writers, and also one of my favourite people, even though we have never actually met. I often seek Michael's thoughts and opinions on work in its early stages, the drafts I wouldn't show anyone else. His advice is always incredibly insightful and his correspondence consistently hilarious. Michael, you're a true friend. An email from you in my inbox never fails to improve the quality of my stories and my day.

To all my beloved friends, thank you for your support and encouragement and for generally being awesome. I feel very lucky in my life to have been blessed with so many close friendships which are still going strong across the decades. Andy Ralston and Tom Mallows — you guys get a special mention here for having read pretty much everything I've churned out and for always finding something nice to say about it. It really does mean a lot.

To my family, who always indulged my creative side, thank you so much. Sorry if I've been a bit of an insufferable smart-arse ever since I started correcting Dad's grammar at age four.

Finally, and most importantly, thank you to my amazing wife,

Sarah. For being your kind, beautiful, funny and caring self. For always inspiring me to want more out of life and for bringing our perfect little girl, Luna, safely into the world. You are the bravest person I know. I'm sorry if I seem distant or self-absorbed from time to time, at least now you'll finally have a detailed and extensive answer to your favourite question, "What you thinking about?" I hope you'll continue asking me after you've read it all.

And finally finally, thanks to YOU dear reader. I hope you have enjoyed spending time with this book. Many of these stories aren't quite finished, and some of the characters are still rather restless. Perhaps you'll want to meet them again, somewhere down the line. And maybe, just maybe, this won't be the last journey we all take together.

Love to you all,

Rick x

ALSO AVAILABLE FROM STORGY BOOKS

PAIN SLUTS

SIAN HUGHES

A teenager performs stripteases in her bedroom window as funeral processions pass by. A grieving mother reunites with her miscarried foetus. A widow takes on the sinister, rapacious treehouse in next door's garden. Combining pitch-perfect, darkly comic observations with tender touches of humanity, Pain Sluts chronicles the flaws, frailties, and enduring spirit of an eclectic cast of curious characters as they navigate threats to their identity and humanity.

A brave and bold literary debut bursting with calamity and compassion, Pain Sluts is an astonishing collection of stories which lays bare our beauty and bizarreness. Laden with love, loss and longing, this book illuminates Sian's extraordinary ability to create believable characters that brave our brittle world, often in outlandish or unusual ways. Sharp and tender, true and wise, these stories announce the arrival of a uniquely talented new voice in British fiction.

To discover more about PAIN SLUTS visit STORGY.COM

ALSO AVAILABLE FROM STORGY BOOKS

PARADE

MICHAEL GRAVES

"Like the Beat Generation writers before him, or Hunter S Thompson's 'Fear and Loathing in Las Vegas', Graves uses a fresh, contemporary, and stylistically original voice to offer darkly comic, satirical perspectives on the false gods of the Great American Dream: celebrity, religion, government, and excessive consumption. But, in the final analysis, Parade's main preoccupation is the question of who we love, what we love, and why: a theme he explores with joy, humanity, hope, and humour."
– Sian Hughes –
Author of *Pain Sluts*

Reggie Lauderdale suffers from a crisis of faith. His cousin, Elmer Mott, dreams of becoming their hometown mayor. Both boys are stuck in suburbia trying to be adults … but they aren't sure how to be themselves yet. When a twist of fate sends them fleeing in a stolen limousine, the cousins escape to Florida where they meet a retired televangelist, who inspires them on a path of glitzy sermons and late-night parties. But are the celebrations sincere or deceptive? And who is keeping tabs? Who is watching? Parade is a tour-de-force, comic tale of faith and friendship.

To discover more about PARADE visit
STORGY.COM

ALSO AVAILABLE FROM STORGY BOOKS

THIS RAGGED, WASTREL THING

TOMAS MARCANTONIO

"A cinematic and theatrical neo-noir painting dripping old-school masters of the genre on to a new canvas using rare concentrated pigments. With beautifully rich backdrops, scenes and characters – it's a real treat for the imagined senses."

– John Bowie –

Bristol Noir

SONAYA NIGHTS - BOOK ONE

Deep in The Rivers, through the winding web of neon alleys, we follow our troubled protagonist, Daganae Kawasaki, as he scours the streets to uncover the truth behind his eleven-year stint in The Heights. But will his search for answers in the dingy basement bars and seedy homework clubs finally distinguish friend from foe, right from wrong, or will he uncover more bitter untruths than ever before? Will he finally find freedom from the pain of his past or will new revelations ignite a lust for revenge? Discover a new voice in modern noir fiction and join Dag on his painful pursuit for salvation and sake.

To discover more about THIS RAGGED, WASTREL THING visit STORGY.COM

ALSO AVAILABLE FROM STORGY BOOK

HOPEFUL MONSTERS

STORIES BY

Roger McKnight

‘Hopeful Monsters’ is one of the best collections of linked stories I’ve ever read.”

– **Donald Ray Pollock** –

Author of Knockemstiff, Devil All The Time, and The Heavenly Table

Roger McKnight’s debut collection depicts individuals hampered by hardship, self-doubt, and societal indifference, who thanks to circumstance or chance, find glimmers of hope in life’s more inauspicious moments. Hopeful Monsters is a fictional reflection on Minnesota’s people that explores the state’s transformation from a homogeneous northern European ethnic enclave to a multi-national American state. Love, loss and longing cross the globe from Somalia and Sweden to Maine and Minnesota, as everyday folk struggle for self-realisation. Idyllic lakesides and scorching city streets provide authentic backdrops for a collection that shines a flickering light on vital global social issues. Read and expect howling winds, both literal and figurative, directed your way by a writer of immense talent.

To discover more about HOPEFUL MONSTERS visit STORGY.COM

ALSO AVAILABLE FROM STORGY BOOKS

SHALLOW CREEK

This is the tale of a town on the fringes of fear, of ordinary people and everyday objects transformed by terror and madness, a microcosm of the world where nothing is ever quite what it seems. This is a world where the unreal is real, where the familiar and friendly lure and deceive. On the outskirts of civilisation sits this solitary town. Home to the unhinged. Oblivion to outsiders.

Shallow Creek contains twenty-one original horror stories by a chilling cast of contemporary writers, including stories by Sarah Lotz, Richard Thomas, Adrian J Walker, and Aliya Whitely. Told through a series of interconnected narratives, Shallow Creek is an epic anthology that exposes the raw human emotion and heart-pounding thrills at the genre's core.

To discover more about SHALLOW CREEK visit STORGY.COM

ALSO AVAILABLE FROM STORGY BOOKS

...EXIT EARTH...

EXIT EARTH delves into dystopian worlds and uncovers the most daring and original voices in print today. With twenty-four short stories, accompanying artwork, afterwords, and interviews, EXIT EARTH is a haunting exploration of the sanity of our species...past, present, and future.

Featuring the fourteen finalists from the STORGY EXIT EARTH Short Story Competition, and additional stories by award winning authors M.R. Carey (The Girl with all the Gifts), Toby Litt (Corpsing, DeadKidSongs), Courttia Newland (The Gospel According to Cane, A Book of Blues), James Miller (Sunshine State, Lost Boys), and David James Poissant (The Heaven of Animals). With accompanying artwork by Amie Dearlove, HarlotVonCharlotte, and CrapPanther.

To discover more about EXIT EARTH visit STORGY.COM

Lightning Source UK Ltd.
Milton Keynes UK
UKHW010606090822
407048UK00001B/239